UNLIMITED EXISTENCE

Unlimited Existence

Joseph Cacciotti

Copyright © 2021 by Joseph Cacciotti.

All rights reserved. No part of this book may be reproduced in any form or by any electronic or mechanical means, including information storage and retrieval systems, without permission in writing from the publisher, except by reviewers, who may quote brief passages in a review.

ISBN: 978-1-956074-75-8 (Paperback Edition)
ISBN: 978-1-956074-76-5 (Hardcover Edition)
ISBN: 978-1-956074-74-1 (E-book Edition)

Book Ordering Information

Phone Number: 315 288-7939 ext. 1000 or 347-901-4920
Email: info@globalsummithouse.com
Global Summit House
www.globalsummithouse.com

Printed in the United State of America

UNLIMITED EXISTENCE

Scientists are certain and have good knowledge, and valid proof on how Dinosaurs apparently met their fate. But the one thing that hasn't been truly discovered is just how long man and woman have been on earth.

If there were truly Cave men back in the Dinosaur era, what happened to them after the asteroid hit the earth. Bones have been discovered but there is no evidence that man was walking around before 28,000 B.C., so the first American immigrants must have arrived after that date.

However, Archeologists have found some new discoveries, and they have discovered cities dug into mountains, caves, and even underground the earth's surface. These discoveries have preceded some of these cities, as far back as the Dinosaur ERA.

Now the big questions are. Did man truly survive the first tsunami, and the ice age? Even though the Pentagon was trying to keep a lid on this underground city discovery, even they couldn't predict, what was about to happen here in this 21st century.

Chapter One

3.5 billion years ago is the earliest known meteor strike to hit the earth, at least four more have been identified to hit the earth in the past 300 million-year-period. This meteor caused the first giant tsunami to sweep around the earth several times, burying everything in its path, and sealing up all the open mountain paths. Everyone assumed that every thing was killed, along with the Dinosaurs, and anything that could have survived the meteor strike, eventually everything would die because, with all the trees and green grass gone. Without their food supply destroyed, they would meet their own fate and either sank into the tar pits, or killed each other for food, and eventually starved to death.

Scientists have figured it would have taken 30 hours, from impact of the tsunami to travel around the earth. Once it reached the end it would collide together and keep bouncing back and forth, spreading several inches of sand and mud all over the earth. The water would have inundated everything but the mountains, and drastically erode the continental land masses. Changing coast lines dramatically and the heat from the meteor would have evaporated, 30 to 300 feet of water in the oceans. It would have killed everything, or almost everything, that was alive at the time on land and near the ocean surface.

There was almost certainly life at this time. Everything primitive, bacterial life and if the meteor impacts were 20 miles in diameter, they would have killed everything on the surface of the Earth. First hot molten rock and water would have withered away most life, and with the massive destruction of the tsunamis would have destroyed even more. Then incredible cold winters, that caused particles in the atmosphere too block out the sun, which would have conspired to kill nearly everything else. Anything that might have survived would have been in deep rocks or below the surface of the Earth.

Shortly after the Meteor and Tsunami strikes approximately 2.6 million years ago, and because of the sun being blocked from the first strike, there was nothing to help keep the earth from freezing up. With no sun or heat the Ice age was soon upon the earth, what ever had lived after the meteor blasts now would soon be frozen.

During the Pleistocene (Ice Age) the Archaic Indians lived during this Holocene epoch, and this would put the Archaic period at about 8,000 B.C. Some scientists think the Archaic Indians could go back as far as 28,000 B.C. After finding the weapons made out of chert stone they used to hunt with, it is believed they may have been from the prehistoric period. Archaic Indians are descendants of the Paleo Indians, and when bones were found in the mountains. Some scientists believed some of these Indians may have survived the ice age, because some of the holes in the mountains were very deep. With some of the drawings they found inside the walls of the mountain regions, this was an indication that these Indians were very intelligent people.

The one big question that is the most puzzling to scientists is, even though the Archaic Indians buried themselves deep inside these mountains. Could they have survived the duration of the Ice Age stage, which lasted over 100,000 years? The end of the last glacial period is believed to have been 12,500 years ago.

Other DNA studies of the American Indian languages and their tooth shapes, all evidence point to the Sub-artic and Artic regions of the western Asia.

Today in the 21st century Detectives John Hammer and Cindy Sharp are in a speedy car chase with a couple of bank robbers. With speeds topping out at nearly 90 miles an hour, it is nearly impossible to shoot out the window of the car. With the crowded streets at this time of day, shooting the tires was out too. Because some innocent by-standers might get hurt, so they have to play it safe.

"Stay with him Cindy, don't let that bum get away from us this time."

"Don't worry John, he might have slipped us up the first time, but now He's ours."

"Hey were in luck, he just drove into the alley behind Row Avenue."

"What makes you think we have him John?"

"Because they're working on the driveway approach on the other end, it's all blocked off, he can't get through," John said laughing.

When they turned into the alley, all they saw was an idling empty car with no driver.

"What's going on here? Where's the driver? Nobody just leaves their car running when they run," John said.

"I don't know John there aren't even any footprints, to indicate which way he ran. Is this guy a ghost?" Cindy asked.

"By the skid marks on the ground, he must have stopped very fast. I figured he thought about running through the barricades, before he stopped, and ran on foot," John said.

"Unless someone else surprised him, and he ran away with them," Cindy said.

"Unless they flew away, how did they leave without us seeing them?" John asked.

"I just wonder what the others will say at the precinct, when we tell them this story," Cindy said.

"Let's go, and get it over with partner, I just hope we have a job left, after we tell the captain what happened," John said.

After dusting for prints, and finding nothing in the car, that might help them with their investigation. They had a few little baggies to hand over to the ballistics squad, and hopefully something would show up, and help back up their story. Silence followed as they headed back to the precinct.

Upon their arrival, instead of being laughed at, they were being praised. They looked puzzled at each other as they heard.

"Hey John, Cindy nice collar, don't know how you caught this guy, we've been after him for months," Detective Sam Stone said.

"What are you talking about?" they asked in unison.

"Hey forget about Batman and Robin, you're the real dynamic duel in my book," Detective Mary Chauffer said.

"Hey John, Cindy can I see you a minute in my office," Captain Stephen Phillips said.

John and Cindy entered the office, and closed the door behind them they sat down in the two chairs in front of his desk.

"First let me commend you for a good collar, and say I put you both up for an accommodation, for the way you handled this collar. We never had as much evidence on anyone like this before, and this Buddy Sewell, will be going away for a very long time, because of you two. What's that in your hand John?" Captain Phillips asked.

"Just a little more evidence, we thought could help this case," Cindy said.

"You can drop it off at the ballistics department when we're done, and all the detectives want to throw a little party together for your collar here today."

"Captain Phillips, we all had a part in getting this scum bag off the streets. I don't feel right us taking all the credit, and not sharing the rewards with everyone in this bureau," John said.

"I second that statement Captain," Cindy said.

"I just knew you two would say that, that's the one thing I admire about the two of you. You're always thinking about the team and not yourselves all the time. Now go take what you have to ballistics, and take the rest of the day off with pay," Captain Phillips said.

Everyone in the precinct started clapping as they stepped out of the office, and both John and Cindy were a little stunned, by what had just happened.

"What's going on here John? I figured we'd be flogged until we cried all the way home. Am I dreaming or is this really happening?" Cindy asked.

"Only one way to find out, let's go drop of this package off in the evidence room, and then check out the prisoner," John said.

Cindy shook her head yes, and together they walked into the evidence room. John went to hand the package over to Slim Stickman, and he looked at them puzzled.

"What are you doing John? You already handed this evidence

to me just about an hour ago. I was able to come up with three sets of prints, one is the original owners. One was the bank robber, and the third I haven't been able to locate as of yet," Slim said.

"What do you mean you can't locate the third set of prints?" Cindy asked.

"I don't understand it either guy's, it's a good clear print. Maybe my machine is a little messed up, and let me try it again since you're here. Maybe I'll have better luck." With that said. Slim set the print back into the scanner.

With-in a few minutes the machine kick off indicating it was done searching, when they looked at the report it read. 'No match found'

"This doesn't make sense Slim I thought everyone in the world, has his print on file today?" John asked

"They are supposed to John, maybe this guy doesn't exist," Slim said.

"What are you saying Slim, that he's dead?" If that's true why dose it show a clear print?" Cindy asked.

"Sorry, but that's one question, I can't answer for you. I can only say, it was a recent print, there's no way it could have been there for years. I wouldn't have been that easy to pick them up then. If you find the answer let us know will you?" Slim asked.

"That's baffling John, what's going on here?"

"Don't know Cindy, but instead of going home after this. I'm going to swing back to where we cornered this guy, and see what we missed the first time."

"I'll go with you John," Cindy said.

Chapter Two

Cindy and John walked out to their car, and just as John sat behind the wheel. There was a strange odor that took over the car, and they both rolled down their windows to breathe some fresh air into their lungs.

"John what the heck is going on here, where did that smell come from?"

"I was going to ask you that same question, I know it wasn't us, or we'd have smelled up the room upstairs.

Cindy turned around, and saw something lying on the back dash near the window.

"John did you have any criminals in the back today?"

"I was with you, why would you ask such a question?"

"Because, if that isn't the case, then someone was inside this car while we were upstairs. They left something in front of the window in the back, and I think they wanted us to find it," Cindy said.

Cautiously, they both stepped out of the car, John opened up the back door. After applying some latex gloves on his hands, he reached in and retrieved the object. When they looked at it close, they noticed the faint smell came from the feathers on the end of this arrow.

"Why would someone put this old arrow inside this car?" John asked.

"John, is that a note taped to the middle of the arrow?" Cindy asked.

"I think we should have this arrow dusted for prints before we go any further, and that goes for touching that note too. Let's go see Shirley in the lab, maybe she can make heads or tails out of this crazy looking arrow,' John said.

As they were headed up the stairs, they ran into Captain Stephen Phillips on the stairway coming down.

"I thought you two were going back to investigate, the so called crime scene area?"

"We started going out there Captain, but we found this hiding in our car," John said handing the bag to Captain Phillips.

"Looks like an arrow John, but it looks like something is wrapped around the neck of it," Captain said.

"Not only that Captain, but if you open that bag, the odor will bring you down to your knees," Cindy said.

Captain Phillips didn't heed their warning, and he opened up the bag. His eyes started watering, and he choked a little for air. "What on earth is that odor from?" Captain Phillips asked.

"We were on our way up, to have Shirley Jacobs take a look at it, maybe she can come up with an idea or two," John said.

"Good thinking, just keep me informed, about what you find."

"Sure will Captain," they said in unison, and headed up to see Shirley Jacobs.

Knocking first, they entered through the door, and saw Shirley working on some other project.

"Hey sweetheart," John said. "Looks like you stay pretty busy these days?"

"Hello John, Cindy, and to what do I owe to this visit?"

"We found this in front of the back window of our car, just a few minutes ago, it stinks to high heaven. It looks like an arrow of some kind, would you have any idea of how old it could be. Maybe it was stolen out of the museum, and left in our car so they wouldn't get caught," John said.

After examining the arrow, Shirley went to her phone and dialed a number.

"Professor Goodyear, this is Shirley Jacobs, from the Racine Police department. I had one of your classes, when you taught here at Gateway Technical College, and I thought you might like to see, what a couple of the officers found inside there car this morning," Shirley said.

"What could they have found, that's so intriguing?" Professor Goodyear asked loud enough for everyone to hear.

"I'm not quite sure, but it looks like an arrow from the Paleo-Indian era," She said.

"'That's impossible they've been instinct since the Ice age era, it must be a replica of some kind," he said.

"Do you have a fax machine, or an email address? Where I can send you some pictures of it, so we can be certain," she asked.

"Yes, I do but it might just be a waist of time, but here's both my fax and e-mail numbers. When will you be sending them to me?" Professor asked.

"They're already on the way Professor I'll hang on, and see what you think. That way I will not have to take up anymore of your time, if you don't mind?" she asked.

"That's quite alright my dear, anytime I can be of assistance don't hesitate to call. I just received them, and no they can't be real. Are you sure you didn't copy these out of a book?" he asked.

"No Professor, it's right here in front of me. There's an odor that is so strong, that it takes your breath away," Shirley said.

"That's because of the smell from that era, Shirley where exactly are you located?" the Professor asked.

After she told him the address, she hung up the phone and said, "We'll see you shortly Professor, and thank you."

"What was that about?" Cindy asked.

"Looks like whoever put this in your car, was an ancient Indian from the past," Shirley said.

"Are you sure this Professor guy isn't a crack-pot, or someone who just lost his marbles. How could that be an ancient arrow from what the Ice Age he said?

"I know it sounds strange John, but what if it is stolen from a museum somewhere? Maybe it's like you said, someone wants to return it without complications," Cindy said.

"Your right Cindy, there's no sense going off half-cocked, until we know for sure, what or who we're dealing with. Let's go down and let the Captain know what's going on,' John said.

"Wait what about the note what does that say?" Cindy asked.

Very slowly and masks and gloves on, they removed the note and passed it around so everyone could read it. *"Since I did you another favor today, I thought you might like to do a favor for me. I will meet you soon."* That's strange it isn't signed.

"Yeah, I can't wait to see what he'll say about all of this?" Cindy said laughing.

"Shirley, please let us know when the Professor gets here?" John asked.

"Since you asked me so nice, how can I say no to that nice request? As soon as he shows up I'll call you," she said.

After reporting to the Captain, Cindy and John went back to the crime scene, to do some more investigating. They saw some of the torn cloth hanging on a few scattered bushes, and then Cindy saw something they must have missed before.

"Hey John, how did we miss this?" Cindy asked.

"What did you find my dear?"

"Looks like some big foot prints, but the question is whose are they? I don't recall seeing these before, and if they were here how could we've missed them?"

"No doubt someone was here after we left, but why were they barefoot? Let's make a cast of these prints, maybe we'll get lucky and finally get a clue," John said.

After mixing the cement and pouring it into the impressions, John's phone started to ring.

'That figures, why is it when you're in the middle of something, the phone always seems to ring?" John asked as he continued to pour in the cement.

Cindy took the phone out of his holder and answered the call. Detective Sharp, how can I help you?"

"Hello Cindy, this is Shirley. Professor Albert Goodyear has just landed, and I'm leaving here now to pick him up. It shouldn't be more than an hour I would say, are you going to come back and meet him?"

"Yes, we are Shirley, we have to wait for some prints to dry and then we'll be there. Thank you for the call," Cindy said hanging up the phone.

"I heard the conversation, and we should be ready to go in about ten more minutes. Thank you for taking the call Cindy."

"Hey that's what partners are for right?" she said.

John grinned and they both broke out in laughter, and that's when John thought he saw someone looking back at them. He took out his binoculars, and when he looked in the direction he couldn't believe his eyes. He wiped his eyes and looked again, but this time he saw nothing. "I must be working to hard," he said under his breath.

"What's wrong John, what did you see?" Cindy asked.

"I thought I saw someone looking back at us, he had a long beard, and scraggly hair down past his shoulders. His eyes looked so dark, but when I wiped my brow and looked again he was gone. I have to go and see if I wasn't just seeing things," John said. As he stood up, he headed into the direction where he saw the person looking back at him. When he made it to where that man would have been, he saw more footprints in the soft dirt around the ground. They went off into the mountain area, and then disappeared. He called Cindy from his phone.

"Hey are those prints hard enough yet?"

"Yes, I'm pulling them out now. Did you find anything?"

"I think so and this could be our missing piece of this puzzle, could you please bring them over here?

Cindy loaded them into the car and drove over where John was, and when she pulled up to him. She noticed a look of bewilderment in his eyes. "What did you find John?"

"Follow me and tell me I'm not dreaming," John said and took one of the molds and headed around the back of the rock.

Cindy followed him without saying a word, figuring she'd understand in a minute what was happening. When she saw the fresh footprints it registered in her mind, and then when the molds fit the new prints.

"Where do they go John?" she asked.

"They disappear behind that rock over there," John said.

"Impossible, how can footprints just disappear?" Cindy said, as she followed the trail which led into a dead end. "Who or what have we stumbled on too?" she said out loud.

"My thoughts exactly, then I'm not losing it. This really did happen, now all I have to do is find out how, and why did it happen," John said.

"Not just you John, I have to know too. This has to be some of kind of sick joke," Cindy said.

John and Cindy saw some crows flying overhead, about twenty-five feet from where they were standing. They motioned to each other to walk over there, and see what the crows were so interested in. They couldn't believe their eyes, as they saw a man lying face down with a spear in his back. But the one thing that boggled their minds was, the dead man, was holding a .45 automatic pistol in his right hand. But they couldn't find any evidence to determine, if that gun had been fired. No shell fragments, no smell or sight of powder burns, John called in a forensic unit and the coroner. They both waited until both parties were present, maybe the coroner could tell them a few things first.

"Did you touch anything before you called us?" Dr. Phyllis Hartman asked.

"No Doctor we left everything, as we found it," Cindy said.

"Looks like he was speared in the back?" Sergeant Harry Meyer said.

"That's the easy part Harry, with that spear sticking out of his back," John said with a smirk on his face.

When Doctor Hartman rolled him over, they found the tip of the spear, sticking out of the other side of his body. "Who ever threw this spear was awfully strong, it pierced straight through, and puncturing his heart too. Hopefully his finger prints will tell us who he is, or was," Doctor Hartman said.

"Doctor, do you have and idea, about when he was killed?" John asked.

"He's still a little warm, and his body hasn't started to decompose yet. I'd say he was killed within approximately two or three hours ago," Doctor Hartman said.

"Shirley, could you please give us a call, when you have something more to go on?" Cindy asked.

"Sure thing Cindy, I must say, I've seen a lot of murders in my career. But this has to be the most bazaar one yet,"

"Shirley, what makes this one any different from all the others?" John asked.

"This is the first one that has been killed by a spear, and there are no gun powder burns on his hand. Either what he saw, scared him so much he couldn't shoot, or he never even saw who his murderer was. I hope to know more when I finish my work on this poor soul," Doctor Phyllis Hartman said.

"How long do you think before you'll know anything Doctor Hartman?" John asked.

"Give me about an hour, and I should have something to get you started at least."

"Thank you Doctor, we'll see you in an hour or so," Cindy said. Then they turned their attention on the forensic team.

"You guys find anything we can use yet?" John asked.

"No it's hard to pinpoint where, or how far the person was, who threw that spear. But as Doctor Hartman said, the person had to be awfully strong. Putting a spear in the back of someone is impressive enough, but to stick it through the man's body. That is what I call scary, if you want to go, we'll let Captain Phillips know if we find anything," Sergeant Sandy Bellows said.

"Thank you Sergeant, let's hope we can close this thing fast," Cindy said and they left.

Chapter Three

"Cindy, before we head back to the precinct, we have to see Shirley Jacobs at her office, and talk with Professor Albert Goodyear, don't tell him what we found here, until we hear what he has to say first," John said. They both agreed and headed back to the lab.

When they arrived at Shirley's office, they weren't surprised to see Shirley standing next to an old grey haired man, looking over the dead body, which they just found a little more than a couple hours ago.

"Shirley saw John and Cindy in the mirror and said. "Good timing you two, I was surprised to find Professor Albert Goodyear at my door, when I returned back from the bathroom. He's been very helpful with this body, and I think you'll find what he's going to tell you is very interesting, and maybe a little hard to believe," Shirley said.

After shaking hands, and making a little chit chat, Professor Goodyear went straight to business.

"I understand that you're the ones who found both, the arrow and the body, did you see anything else besides these two findings?" Professor Goodyear asked.

"Yes we did Professor, Cindy and I thought we saw someone watching us, when we went back to look around some more at the crime scene. But when we went to investigate what we saw, we didn't find anybody there, but we did find footprints in the soft sand. We made some cement molds of them, and here they are," John said.

As Cindy opened up the brief case, they pulled them out, and handed them to Shirley and the Professor. Professor Goodyear's eyes grew like silver dollars, and he looked like he saw a ghost. Slowly his scared look started to change, and his frown was now replaced with a wide smile.

"You say you took these today?" the Professor asked.

"Yes, just before we found the body. Why do you ask?" Cindy

asked.

"Because, whoever this person is. He likes you, and he's trying to help you."

"What are you talking about Professor Goodyear, who's trying to help us?" John asked.

"Let me start at the beginning, so you understand me better. During, the last glacial age, or more known to us as the ice age. 10,000 or 12,000 years ago, when the Dinosaurs still roamed this earth.

The Paleoindians were the first known people to live in the Americas, including Indiana. These early people lived in small groups, of related individuals and moved around a lot, they hunted large game animals, including the extinct Mastodon, a large elephant-like creature. They also lived off wild plants to eat for survival.

The Paleoindians, made their own weapons, and were well-made stone tools. The types of stones were called chert, which was afine-grained rock that breaks a little glass when hit by hard materials like another rock or a piece of deer antler. The tools they made were made by chipping, flintnapping, and flaking included long spearpoints, cutting and scraping implements, and engraving items. Some of their spear and piercing tools are called Clovis, Cumberland, Quad, Plainview, Hi-Lo, and Agate Basin Points.

Evidence to some of these people have been found in Indiana on land near water sources like major rivers and springs, and where chert is found. Little is known about the Paleoindians since they moved around and didn't occupy any one place for long. They didn't leave behind much evidence of their lives in any one place. But they have found evidence that they once lived beneath the earth during the glacier age. Today they are still discovering many hidden underground caves, that we never knew existed."

"That sounds interesting Professor, but what exactly is chert?" John asked.

"Chert, is a very dense type of quartz, including jasper and flint. Not only is this quartz rock, strong enough to penetrate a Dinosaurs tough hide, it can also be used for making fire. That's how intelligent these Indians were even back in those days," Professor Goodyear said.

"So you're saying that we may have stumbled on to, an ancient arrow that was probably stolen from the museum?" Cindy asked.

"It's an ancient arrow alright, but it wasn't made back in those days. This is relatively a new arrow, do you see how straight this arrow is. The arrows made back in the prehistoric days, were slightly bowed. Due to the fact they made the arrows out of any type of tree limbs they could reach, unless they were able to climb the tree," the Professor said.

"If it isn't an old arrow, where did it come from?" John asked.

"We heard that Doctor Phyllis Hartman had a body, and the person was speared through the heart. I asked her if I could examine the body myself, and since I didn't feel right going into a morgue at my age. She said she would have the body brought here, and she would pick it back up tomorrow. I asked her to bring the spear along with the body, and unless I'm mistaken. This man was killed because of something he did that made someone very mad."

"Well I didn't think the person had feelings for him, when he sent a spear clear through his back and out his heart," John said sarcastically.

"I heard a little buckshot in that statement detective, and let me explain this a little easier for you. I've studied the Paloindians, since I found out about them back in grade school, and I must say, that even though we've never seen these Indians, it doesn't mean they didn't exist."

"Professor, Are you saying that these Indians still exist after all these years?" Cindy asked.

"That's one possibility, after all there were many different tribes assembled in those days. They all went their own way, and the Cherokee's, Sioux, and Apache were all a part of the beginning of man. Which included many tribes before and after the Ice age, and these men were what we called, cave men back then. Isn't it impossible that some of these tribes could still exist today?" Professor Goodyear asked.

"Yes, many tribes are still alive Professor, but they all live on what we call reservations today. Not to mention all the gambling casinos," John said.

"I'm not talking about the Indians that we found on the surface of the earth, but what if some of them do exist, under this planet we call earth today?"

"That's impossible, isn't it?" Cindy asked. "Nobody could exist underground that long could they?"

"The total ice age lasted nearly 100 years, and we've found some cities underground recently that were used back in those days. Those people lived in the ground, and they probably know the underground, better than we'll ever know the surface of this earth."

"I understand what you're saying professor, but do you really think this is possible?" Cindy asked.

"The man you thought you saw, what did he look like exactly?" the Professor asked.

"From what I could see through my binoculars, he looked like he was a big man. He had very large shoulders, and his long hair was past his shoulder blades. He didn't run right away, but he disappeared very fast. He moved like a gazelle, and we never saw him up to close or where he ran too," John said.

"He wanted to get your attention, because he's probably the one who killed this man."

"You're kidding right Professor, he never had a weapon on him," Cindy said.

"Are you sure he didn't have a weapon?"

"All we saw was a bamboo stick at the scene," Cindy said.

"Was the stick hallowed out?"

"Yes, Professor it was, but how would you know that?" Cindy asked.

"Because that was his weapon, they carve out the center of the bamboo sticks. They attach a piece of vine from a tree inside the tube. They take a spear, and insert it into the bamboo stick with some of the vine sticking out. Then they pull it tight against the vine, and then quickly release it to there target. They are very good archers, and they very seldom miss their targets,"

"That sounds like a bunch of bull to me professor," John said.

"Do you have the bamboo stick with you?"

"Yes it's out in the vehicle, we were going to take it to forensics for fingerprints after we stopped here, why do you ask?" John asked.

"Can I see it please?" the Professor asked.

John, went to the car, and brought the bamboo stick back into the room. He handed the stick to the professor; he cautiously looked it over and found the vine he had talked about tucked inside. Pulling the vine out, the professor took the spear, and inserted it into the bamboo sick. Grabbing the string he inserted the spear into the tube, and then he looked around for a target. His eyes caught on a little target bulls eye on the bathroom door.

"Watch, this kids, and learn something new," he said.

Professor Goodyear pulled back the spear, and held onto the vine, when the spear was tight. He brought his arm straight aiming toward the door, the spear shot out like it was fired from a high powered gun, and the spear went through the door. Everyone was stunned as they opened the door, and saw the spear sticking through the medicine cabinet. They felt lucky because, had that medicine cabinet not been there. The spear may have gone through the wall and hit an innocent by-stander.

"You just made me a believer Professor, but if they do exist. How can we find them?" John asked.

"You will not find them, but they will find you, when the time is right. Whoever that was by those rocks wanted to meet you, or he wouldn't have waited until you were almost on him. Maybe if you go back there a few more times, he might just feel more comfortable, to come out and talk to you," Professor Goodyear said. "This footprint you brought back, tells me this man you're chasing. Stands approximately six foot two or bigger, and might weigh around two hundred and fifteen pounds."

"How, can a man that big disappear that fast, without a trace of where he went?" Cindy said.

"Remember, if he came from under the earth. He knows every crevice in the rocks to escape through. I think in time, he will eventually show you where he lives, and please be patient, and don't push him into a corner. If you make him mad, and then you'll never find out who he is. But I think you two have found a friend," Professor Goodyear said.

Chapter Four

"John, I don't know about you, but I'm a little curious, about just who was behind those rocks watching us. But what really bothers me, is we weren't that far behind him when he ran toward the rocks. Why couldn't we see where he disappeared too, it's almost like he vanished into thin air?"

"I understand what you're saying, and if I hadn't seen it with my own eyes, I'd think you were crazy telling me this. But now, I'm also having trouble, trying to figure it out. In all my years on the force, I've never been as bewildered by a case, like this one. Not to say we haven't had our share of bad moments, but at least we had a clue as to what happened to those two people. However, in this case, we have no fingerprints, strange weapons found, no robbery attempt, and a secret admirer we can't find. I begin to wonder, what have we've became involved with here. Plus now that we know what was used, to make that spear go clean through a body, and straight through the man's heart. Who ever we're after he's either a master at his craft or a lucky shot. I've been thinking, if he's targeting us, I don't think either one of us should be alone, until this guy, or people are caught," John said.

"I think you're right John, but we both have a home to go to. So we'll be alone for a few hours to sleep," Cindy said.

"Hey partner, we're both divorced, and live alone. There's nobody there to watch our backs, so what do you think, about sleeping over at my place until this is over?"

"John, why should I sleep at your place, what's wrong with you sleeping at my house?"

"Cindy, I have three bedrooms at my place, one is my office the other is a spare bedroom for guests. It's not being occupied at this time, and I think it'll work out better for us," John said.

"John, I also have three bedrooms, with a sewing room of my own. The other is unoccupied too, and you're welcome to use it. So what makes your place any better than mine?" Cindy asked.

"For one thing, my house is completely fenced in all around the back, and the only way they could come in is through the front door. With the bedrooms toward the back of the house, we'd have plenty of time to hear them coming and get ready for who ever it is."

"Ready for whom John, we don't even know if anyone is coming after us at this point. If you remember right, this person wasn't scared of us. If he or they wanted to kill us, they could have done it before we called anyone to the crime scene," Cindy said.

"I was an eagle scout when I was younger, and I believe in one of the motto's we had. "Be prepared" Why wait until it's too late to worry about it besides, I have a little indoor swimming pool inside my place."

"John, are you that rich? When did you have a pool put into your house?"

"Not rich Cindy dear, it was in already when I bought the house. The couple I bought the house from said, they were too old to enjoy it anymore. I have to admit it's come in handy, when I needed to soak my soar body, it seems to relax me before I go to bed."

"We'll you make it hard to say no John, but who will I get to watch my place, when I'm sleeping over at your place?"

"Maybe you could ask one of the single women at the precinct, if they want a temporary place to stay for a few days?" John asked.

"That might not be a bad idea after all, ever since my divorce. I've been looking for someone to help me with the payments, and if they work out, who knows. I just might find someone to help me around the house, but what do I say the reason is?" Cindy asked.

"Tell them the truth, and that you're on a special assignment. That you have to leave your house for a few days, and you need someone to watch your place. Let them know that you're looking for a possibly roommate, to help with the bills and chores," John said.

"You know, John, I think that could work for me. Thank you for putting this thought in my mind, and maybe tomorrow, we can go back to the site, and see if we missed anything," Cindy said.

"We can do that, if we go early enough, maybe we can finally hook-up with the guy, who doesn't want to be found," John said.

"Since we have that settled. If I'm staying at your place for a few days, I need to get a few things from my house. Unless you have any objections," Cindy said.

"My thoughts exactly, I have a few boxes at my place if you need them."

"John, how much stuff do you think I need for a few days?"

"It depends, how long those few days stretch out to be, my dear," John said.

"I don't plan on staying by your place that long, besides I think we'll find this guy tomorrow, and it'll all be over," Cindy said.

When they arrived at Cindy's house, John helped pack her hair dryer, and few other essentials women need. Cindy was busy, packing some of her clothes into her suit cases, and before she was finished. She pack her swim suit, and was hoping John wasn't kidding her about his pool. She could use something to relax her, after the day they have had today.

John complemented Cindy, on her choice of colors and decor, around the house. Besides, John and Cindy being partners for almost two years, except for working together and being divorced. They never really knew much about each other, and they were both a little nervous. Because, since some of their colleagues knew they were divorced, and probably vulnerable, they'd have to be ready to be ridiculed at work, about what they were doing every night living together. But they both knew it was easier, and safer to do this. Than worrying about what could happen, and not getting any sleep.

"Hey John, do you want to stop off somewhere for a drink or two, and take the edge off our minds before we get to your place?" Cindy asked.

"Great suggestion partner, I think we're both a little jittery, about what the others will think from this day forward," John said.

"Yeah, some children never grow up," Cindy said.

They both laughed and headed for the first bar they saw, and they pulled into Joey's Tavern on highway 32. Being strangers to this place, all eyes were on them as they sat down in a booth. John asked Cindy what she wanted, and headed for the bar.

"Bartender, a couple bottles of Miller light please, nice place you have here. I've always drove past your place, but this is the first time I stopped. I'll have to visit you more often," John said.

"Thank you mister, my name is Joey Cantrell, I'm the owner of this tavern," he said as he extended his hand for a friendly shake.

"My name is John Hammer, and my partner over there is Cindy Sharp. It's a pleasure to meet you Joey," John said.

"Partner, as in a couple or," before Joey continued John held up his hand.

"We're detectives, nothing kinky here, we work together," John said.

"You must be a fool John," Joey said.

"What are you talking about Joey?"

"Unless you're a blind man, she's a beautiful looking woman. If you don't watch yourself, this could turn into something, much more serious my new friend," Joey said.

"Yes, I agree with you Joey, she has a lovely face, and a smile that could melt your heart. But we are professionals, we work together solving crimes," Johns said.

"You know John, if I wasn't married. I'd be trying to make that lovely creature mine. If you pass up an opportunity like that, you should get your head examined."

When John made it back to the table, John was now more aware, as to the beauty in Cindy's face. She saw him looking into her eyes, in a way he's never looked at her before.

"You were up there a long time, looks like you made a new friend," Cindy said.

"Yes, I did, we had a good conversation. He's a very intelligent man, who knows how to read people," John said.

"What did you guy's talk about?"

John almost said it, but he caught himself before he said Cindy's name. "He just thought he knew me from somewhere else, but it turned out I wasn't the guy he was thinking about. Now what are we going to do, about our surprised guest this evening, I wonder if he'll be there tomorrow," John said.

"I'm just wondering, where he came from at this point," Cindy said.

"Hopefully, we'll find out more tomorrow, I think the earlier we get there, the better chance we have of finding our new found friend," John said.

Cindy, was about to say something, when the song from Ghost came on the jukebox. When John saw Cindy swaying to the music, he thought about it before he asked.

"Would you like to Dance?"

"I'd love to," Cindy said. As they walked out on the floor, John looked over at Joey, and he had a wide grin on his face. John was set up, and he knew Joey was the culprit. He had to admit that Cindy, sure felt and smelled good as he held her in his arms, close to his body. John was getting some strange thoughts in his mind, like maybe the two of them together alone in his house. Was not a logical thing to do, but then he thought this was just a dance nothing more. But why did he feel butterflies in his stomach, holding Cindy so close to him. When the song ended they finished their drinks and headed out the door.

"Joey, this is my partner Cindy," John said as he introduced the two of them.

"Cindy if you don't mind my saying, you're a very beautiful woman. You're both welcomed back into my tavern anytime, have a great night you two," Joey said as they exited the door.

Chapter Five

John helped Cindy, take her things into his house, and it dawned on him, that this was the first woman he has had inside this house, since his divorce. He couldn't stop thinking, that it was almost five years ago, and he's never even looked at another woman, the same way he did before he was married. Now, as he followed Cindy inside his house, even with her uniform on. He couldn't help but notice the sway of her hips, and even though he kept telling himself, he had no emotional feelings for her. He wondered what she looked like underneath that uniform, and he was hoping, he would find out real soon.

After Cindy was unpacked, and getting used to her new surroundings, she put on her two piece bathing suit, and walked out of her room. John was busy trying to find something in the kitchen to make for dinner. Cindy thought he would hear her coming, but when he never turned around.

"John, could you point me in the direction of your pool. I think I'll take a little swim, to help me relax these tired old bones?" she asked.

When John turned to point the way, his eyes nearly came out of their sockets. His mouth was open, but nothing was coming out. He saw Cindy standing in front of him with her two piece bathing suit, and her hour glass figure and perky breasts, were teasing him.

"The pool is just past those double doors to the right," he finally said.

"What, do you want me to swim alone, dinner can wait? What if I slip and fall by the pool," Cindy said with a wide smile on her face. As she headed for the pool, she heard John fumbling around in the kitchen.

He headed into his bedroom, like a high school boy on his first date, and he downed his clothes and put on his trunks. He was trying to calm his beating heart, he had wondered before what Cindy looked like out of her uniform, and now he was scared to death about what might happen in the next couple days. She was the complete package 36-24-36 and as close to a ten as he's ever seen. John was feeling like a high school kid again, and he was hoping with the way he was feeling, he wouldn't do something stupid and scare her away.

When John entered the pool room, Cindy was standing in the shallow side of the pool.

"About time John, I thought you didn't want to swim with me," Cindy said.

Cindy was standing inside the pool, with her hair all wet, and her perky big nipples pushing against her halter top. John felt the fire inside him starting to burn, and had to dive in fast, before he embarrassed himself. He couldn't believe how his blood pressure shot up, but he wasn't expecting Cindy to have a killer body like this. He stayed under water until he was in front of Cindy, and came up to stand in front of her.

Cindy noticed the look in his eyes, and she also had a hard time looking away from John too. John's body was chiseled with muscles, from all the weight lifting he does at work. Cindy felt the burning in her body too, it was like a magnet was trying to pull them close, neither one wanted to make the first move. Until John took Cindy's hand in his, he saw the hurt in her eyes before he said.

"It's not that I don't want to hold you close, but I think we should take it a little slow for now. It's been almost five years, since I last kissed another woman, and I don't want to scare you away. We've been partners way too long, to mess it up now."

"John, I knew this was a mistake, maybe I should go back home. I've been alone for three years myself, and I apologize to you, I don't know what came over me. I wasn't trying to take advantage of you. I've never had feelings for anyone like this, for a very long time."

"Cindy, are you saying, you're in love with me?"

"Not up until these last couple months, I noticed how you took care of me, and yourself. You're a very good Detective, and you're willing to train me with dignity and trust. I was scared of you at first, but you have a soothing way, about how you conduct business. I'm honored to have you as my partner for the past two years, but I was scared of doing this, because it might be too much for us to handle. It might force us to break up as a team, and that is something I couldn't handle. That was why I was reluctant to stay by your house, when you first asked me," she said.

"I've feelings for you too Cindy, I wasn't sure how much, until I saw you in your bathing suit. I haven't seen anyone, as beautiful as you in a very long time, and I was afraid. I'd do something stupid, like a high school boy and scare you off. It's been such a long time since I felt anything this strong for anyone, and I wasn't sure how you would re-act if I came on too strong."

Cindy pulled John into her arms, wrapped her arms around his neck. Then slowly pressed her lips against his, it took a couple times, but John finally started kissing her back. When John started to massage her back, he found the loop of her tank top. Slowly he untied it, and felt her soft breasts against his own chest.

Cindy purred a little, and pressed her body closer to Johns, as she felt him growing under the water. Slowly, she reached down and worked his trunks off his hips, and then she pulled the side ties on her suit, and now they were both naked in the pool. Wrapping her legs around his hips, she felt John lift her into place. And soon they were in another world, and when John felt Cindy, start too slid up and down into a smooth rhythm. He grabbed her small waist and helped her momentum, and they never broke their passionate kissing even after they were satisfied. Their lips were still locked together, as John carried her back to his bedroom.

When John sat down on the bed, Cindy stayed locked around his waste. As he sat down Cindy gave a moan, as he penetrated her a little farther. She was happy when she felt the affect it was having on John, they weren't going to be getting much sleep tonight.

When Cindy opened her eyes, she thought about what happened last night, and she wondered if it was just a dream. Until she saw John's eyes looking back into hers, her smile told John all he had to know. John had no intensions of this happening, and he was about ready to apologize when he heard.

"John, I'm not sure what came over us last night, but I must admit, I haven't felt this way about anyone else in a very long time. What we did last night was incredible,"

"I never thought I'd ever meet anyone else, who could make me feel this way again. I had no intensions of taking advantage of you, while you were here. I apologize for that," John said.

"John, what are you talking about, you didn't take advantage of me. It was me who seduced you, after all I invited you to join me for a swim remember."

"I'm not sure how this is going to affect us working together."

"What are you talking about John?"

"I don't know if I could think of you, as just my partner anymore, not after what we just did. I can't believe this has happened to me again, but I think I really have strong feelings for someone again, and they are all for you."

"As I do for you John, but let's not throw away a good partnership. Just think in the daytime we're partners in crime, and at night we're partners in life. That's if you still want to continue seeing each other after this?" Cindy asked.

"There's nothing else I'd rather do, it's just that, I don't want it to get old, if we spend almost twenty-four hours a day together. I already lost someone five years ago from not seeing her, will the same thing happen to me, if we see each other all the time, at work and play?" John asked.

"If it gets to be too much, we can always ask for a change of partners. Who knows if it gets really serious, they'll probably split us up anyway? To much emotional involvement," Cindy said.

"Are we getting a bit carried away here now? Let's go find our mystery guest, and find out what the heck is going on.

"First we have to release each other, so we can get dressed. But it feels so good I don't really want to let go," Cindy said.

Slowly John pulled away from Cindy, and he had to admit she was right. He wanted to just stay in bed all day with Cindy too, but first they had to find the man of the hour.

"Cindy, I'll go and start breakfast, how do you like your eggs?"

"Scrambled, smothered with American cheese mixed with it."

"Would you settle for Cheddar cheese, it's still yellow?" John asked.

"That'll be fine John, thank you for asking. Now let me go so I can get ready, or we'll never get out of this bed. Not that I'd complain about it," she said.

"Alright, take your time you have ten minutes, before breakfast is served."

"It'll only take me seven for Cindy to shower, and get ready, and don't let the eggs get cold before I get back." Cindy said. As she ran into her room to get a change of clothes, and she was sitting at the table in seven minutes flat. John was now serving the food and they finally both sat down.

"It smells great John, were did you learn to cook like this?"

"I cooked back when I was a boy scout, and since my divorce, it was either learning how to cook or starve. As you can see I succeeded in the cooking department," John said.

"John, what's that piece of paper on your refrigerator for?" Cindy asked.

"John hadn't noticed it before, but there it was almost in front of him. He peeled the note off the refrigerator, and read it out loud. *'I've been following you and your partner, meet me at the crime scene at ten o'clock today. Don't be late.'*

"Who is this guy? How'd he get into the house without us hearing him? What have we stumbled on to?"

"Settle down John, did you have any windows open you could have forgotten about?"

"No I checked all the windows, before I came out to the pool. Didn't want any intruders, when we were swimming," John said.

"Then we'll have to ask him, when we see him at ten right?" Cindy asked.

"Hey it's almost seven o'clock, if we have to be at the office by eight. We better start getting dressed, that is unless you want to play hooky today?' John asked.

"Even if we play hooky, we still have to meet this mystery/man at ten o'clock. Knowing our luck, this could last all day, and then we'd have wasted a perfectly good hooky day," Cindy said.

"Why don't you go, and start getting ready, I'll do dishes and put them away when we get back later," John said.

"Sounds good to me, just tell me something. It's been so long since I made love, how was I," Cindy asked.

"You were magnificent my dear, but it is I who should have asked you this question. After all I've been suffering for the past five years, but I must admit except for some tired legs. I feel great and full of energy," John said.

Within a half hour, John and Cindy were heading into work, when John noticed his door wasn't closed tight. Knowing he closed and locked it the night before, he started to feel around the underside of his car. Cindy joined in and they were looking to see if someone had wired the car. After finding nothing wrong, they opened the door and sat down. John and Cindy saw the note pasted on his steering wheel which read '*In case you missed the one in the house, meet me at ten o'clock at the crime scene by the mountain. Please if you bring anyone else along, besides the two of you, you'll never see me again.*'

"Well at least we know one thing about our new friend."

"What is that John?"

"He can sure get into some awful tight places without making a sound, and I don't know if that makes him or her a very good thief, or a ghost from the past coming back to help us finish a case,"

"Sometimes John, I think you watch too much television, you probably saw that on those old Twilight Zone movies on the oldies station," Cindy said.

John smile a little at that remark, as they pulled up to the precinct. John parked the car. he couldn't help stop thinking about this mystery/person, that they would soon meet.

When John and Cindy saw they had ten minutes before the briefing, they decided to let the Captain know what was going on later today.

"I don't know if going alone is the right call guy's, after all we know nothing about this guy. It could be a trap, and he's trying to deceive all of us, so he can kill you," Captain Phillips said.

"Well if he wanted to kill us, he could have slit our throats last night, when he came into my house. The one thing that really bothers me Captain, is how did he get in and not make a sound," John said.

"Do me one favor John, when you get to your destination, call me on your cell phone, and stick it in your pocket, but don't hang up. I'll have the other guys waiting close by, in case you need help, Captain Phillips said.

"Very smooth trick Captain, this must be why, they pay you the big bucks," John said.

"We'll clue the others in and set it up, we don't have much time, so let's get out there and let them know what's about to go down."

"After Captain Phillips, was finished clueing the others into what was about to happen, they all seemed to volunteer to help out. This made John and Cindy breathe a little easier, knowing they weren't going in totally alone. John was just hoping the mystery man, wouldn't see the others setting up around them.

Chapter Six

John and Cindy were sitting on the hill, as they were instructed to do, and they were hoping who ever this person was, didn't see their colleagues following far behind them. John kept looking at his watch, and Cindy was a bit fidgety herself.

"Where is this guy, do you think he saw the others behind us?" Cindy asked.

"Relax Cindy, there are still four minutes left, before we know he stood us up," John said.

Then they saw a flash about forty yards farther down, from where they were, only problem was because of the rough terrain, and the big rocks, they would have to walk from here.

"Alright Cindy, lets go meet our mystery guest shall we," John said.

They both exited the car, John opened up his coat. Took out his weapons, put them up in the air to show him he was unarmed, and then he put them in the car, and closed the door.

"John, are you crazy? What happens if this is a trap," Cindy said.

"If he's the person who threw that spear, he could have killed us anytime he wanted too. I don't think his intentions are to harm either one of us," John said.

"I hope you're right," Cindy said, as she put her gun in the car along with John's.

"Besides, I always have my back up strapped around my ankle handy, just in case."

Cindy smiled a little, as they began their walk toward the stranger waiting by the rocks. John was thinking he would disappear before, they met up with him again, but this time he wasn't moving.

At first they thought it was a manikin, dressed up to fool them. Until he gave them a little smile, and just when, they were a few feet from him, he motioned with his hand for them to follow him.

John and Cindy couldn't believe the size of this person, he must have stood 6'6". He was very muscular, and maybe two hundred-fifteen pounds tops, he had very broad shoulders. He was also wearing blue jeans and a short sleeve shirt, John and Cindy never spoke to him, as they followed close behind. Suddenly, he stopped and motioned for them to continue to follow him, together they walked inside this hole in the mountain they never knew existed.

"Hey! Wait a minute pale, we don't even know you yet, and you want us to follow you inside this mountain. Do you think we're crazy?" John said.

"No John Hammer, I don't think you or Cindy Sharp, are crazy. I think you are very good warriors, and that is why I've chosen to work with you," he said.

"Wait, how is it you know our names, but we don't know anything about you?" Cindy asked.

"But you do know me, and I've been helping you out, for the past four years John. Do you remember the clues you were finding, for the past six murders before this last one?" I even helped you, with the man you were chasing the other day, I'm sorry I couldn't have spoken to you earlier. I was there when Cindy joined you about two years ago, and I waited until I figured you were comfortable with another partner. John, are you glad she's working with you? He asked.

"Clues, what are you talking about buddy?" John asked.

"Do you remember the red sneaker by the dead girls' body, or the torn sweat shirt by that young boy who tragically was beaten to death? You would have never have solved those cases, had I not found those items for you. Then there was the broken glasses, form that rapped teacher, the unmarked gun from the bank robbery. The missing neck tie from the last strangulated priest." He said.

"Wait! Are you telling me, you've been helping us solve these cases?" John asked.

"I think that is exactly what he's telling us John, and I bet he has a good reason for killing that man two days ago, don't you sir?" Cindy asked.

"He was about to get away with taking a little child, I couldn't let him get away with that boy. He would have tortured, and then killed him, and you would have been too late to stop him."

"So you're the one who threw that spear, and left the arrow in our car?" John asked.

"The arrow was supposed to get your attention, to find the body along these hills. As you see it worked, and I had no time to retrieve my spear, before you showed up," he said.

"Why didn't you talk to us then?" Cindy asked.

"Too many people would have seen me, and there were two of them, I didn't trust," He said.

"Speaking of trust, you know our names, and everything about us. But we don't know

anything about you and for starters, what is your name?" John asked.

"I'm called Austenaco where I come from, and Andy, when I'm walking on your land," he said.

"What do you mean walking on our land?" Cindy asked.

"It is better if I show you were I come from because, you will not believe me if I tell you," Austenaco said.

"Try us where do you come from?" John asked.

"From inside the rocks," Austenaco said.

"You're right we don't believe you, you better show us," Cindy said.

"Then follow me," Austenaco said. He turned and headed in between two more rocks.

John and Cindy followed close behind the Chief, and they observed as the rocks seemed to open up in some areas. They saw little waterfalls inside some of the caves, and when John cupped his hands to get a drink, the water was pure and clean. Then as if they were looking at a picture book, the greenest grass they ever saw came into sight. There were areas that corn and other vegetables, were growing tall and strong.

"Cindy, pinch me, and tell me this isn't a dream," John said.

"Funny, I was just going to ask you the same thing," she said.

They entered a little patch of trees, and there in the middle of the trees, stood a teepee. Not to far away, he saw a little creek with clear running water, and sitting next to the teepee was an older Indian with a full headdress. John figured he must be the big chief, and he looked like he was older than the hills. He stood as he saw Austenaco with two white people walking behind him.

They both gave hand signals as Austenaco moved in closer, and then they shook hands and talked in their native tongue. John thought everything was good until the big chief pointed at Cindy, and then said something, and what ever Austenaco said calmed him down fast.

"This is Head Chief Yonaguska, he's are leader, and was surprised that women in your world are working like the men."

"What do you mean our world Austenaco? Are we not still here on earth?" Cindy asked.

"In our world there is still purity, the water is good for drinking out of the rivers. The air is cleaner, and we have no pollution, or worries about how we live. We are the same as when we first were born into our world, and now your world is full of hatred and deceit. The people in your world would rather kill each other than help," Austenaco said.

"Don't be ridicules because, all we did is walk between some rocks. What is the difference between here, and outside these caves," John said.

"When you walked between those rocks, you entered a whole new dimension that you know nothing about. This is the earth, but you are in the middle of the earth," Austenaco said.

"What do you mean in the middle of the earth?" Cindy asked.

"Our ancestors were here, way before anyone else walked the earth, and they were the Paleo- Indians. They walked upon this earth, back when the mighty Dinosaurs walked this earth. They lived through the Ice era, and that lasted over 100,000 years. They survived because they learned how to live under ground, they learned how to eat, hunt and survive in the coldest of time. There are still many tribes, scattered all over this world living underground today. The white man, call them Cavemen in the books I've read," Austenaco said.

"If what you say is true, that the Paleo Indians were the first here on earth then, how can there be so many different tribes?" John asked.

"I was told by my ancestors, when the earth started getting darker and colder. Many people in the tribe split up and went their own way, and back then there were a little more than 200 tribes scattered among this earth. Now because of some tribes who have become instinct, we have around 116 tribes left," Austeaco said.

"Are you saying that all except eighty-four tribes are still in the United States, from your ancestors from the ice age, and that sounds so incredible to me? Are they living in the underground like you?" John asked.

"Yes, there are some that still live in the caves underground this earth, but many have been taken off their land, and put into reservations, as the white man calls them today. But instead of splitting them up, there are some reservations that have, the Cherokee's Arapaho, Chippewa (Ojibwa), Dakota (Sioux), Navajo, and the Apache among many others living together on the land. What was once our land and plenty of wild life is now split up, and all of the animal's homes have all been destroyed, just like our homes were. Your water is no good for drinking anymore, unless you put chemicals in it to make it clean. Ours is still the purest in the streams, and we have plenty of food to eat and keep us happy," Austenaco said.

"Then why did you kill that man on the other side of the rocks?" Cindy asked.

"There was a group of men who found a way into our world, and how they found us I do not know. While I was out hunting for food they found my wife Tayanita, and my son Mohe. By the time I arrived back home, I found my wife naked and bloody, and my youngest son was cradled in her arms, they were both dead. I found their tracks, and followed them out the way they came in. When I exited the rocks, I saw one man standing by his car. He raised his gun to shoot, but nothing came out. That is when he tried to run, but nobody can outrun my spear when I throw it. Soon after I threw it, I saw your lights, and thought you were part of his group. When I saw you were not, I decided to help you out," Austenaco said.

"Why don't you come along with us and explain what happened, since it was self defense. I can guarantee you nothing will come out of this, you will be free to come back to your home," John said.

"But I can not go with you now, not until I justify my families killing. I must find these other men and kill them."

"Austenaco, we can't let you do that. We'll find them, and justice will be served to these scumbags. But we can't allow you to go around like a vigilante, and take matters into you own hands," John said.

"I'm not asking to go alone, I would like to team up with you, and we can help each other find them together. Besides, I'm the only one who knows what they look like," Austenaco said.

"What if we said no to your request?" John asked.

"Then I will say good buy to you now, and go find them myself."

"How can you go after them, when you live inside this mountain?" Cindy asked.

"The same way I learned to talk your language, I went to school in your world and learned how to drive a car. I even own my own car, and I've been living in your world for the past fifteen years. Looking for these men, and it will only take me a little time to find them. Because, I have found someone, who knows the names of these men I am looking for."

"How did you get anyone to tell you anything?" Cindy asked.

"At first, he was very resistant to answer any questions, until I threatened to cook him over a fire pit, and feed him to the dogs, bones and all. He told me of many bad men out there, who do this kind of thing all the time. That's when I came up with this idea of working with the two of you, when I find out whom, and where these people are. I will contact you and wait, for you to come and arrest them. But I will only give you so much time, and if you don't make it on time, then I will have to take matters in my own hands. While you're on your way here, you might want to call an ambulance, or better yet the morgue limo."

"Austenaco, you just can't make that decision to take someone's life, they have rights," Cindy said.

"He did have rights, but he gave up those rights. After he decided to rape and murder my family, I feel the right punishment should equal, the wrong they have done."

"Austenaco, I understand what you're saying, and after thinking about what you're asking. If we do work together, I want an understanding between us. If you find someone, you call us immediately, and unless there's nothing else you can do, and he looks like he could be gone before we get here. You have our permission to take matters into your own hands, but this is to apprehend the person in question. We must first find out if they are who you think they are. Before anyone gets killed, because if you step over that line Austenaco, we will have no choice but to come after you, so let's just say this is just a trial period," John said.

"Accepted, we will be very good for each other," Austenaco said.

"John! What the hell is wrong with you, you just can't make a deal with this man, until we get a clearance with the Captain. You could lose your badge over this," Cindy said.

"I understand that Cindy, but Austenaco has a point, he has eyes all over this town. He can find people faster than we can, and if you elect to find someone else as a partner. I will not hold anything against you, but I'm getting tired of putting these guys behind bars. Just to let them walk out on the other side, and go back to killing one more time. How are you going to call us when you find someone?" John asked.

"I'll go find the nearest pay phone," Austenaco said.

"That will not do, here take my extra cell phone. I'll drop

off my charger later on today, my number for my phone is on there, and remember if you find someone, call before you do anything. Are we under an agreement here?" John asked.

"Yes John we are, but I must ask you just one more thing. If someone should ask you how you're getting this information, you tell them nothing about me. I want to remain anonymous, nobody must know our true identity," Austenaco said.

Chapter Seven

On their way back to the precinct, John and Cindy were trying to figure out how they would explain this to Captain Phillips. They just couldn't say Austenaco was an underground dweller, and then Cindy suddenly perked up.

"Hey John, what if we tell the Captain, that this guy is a bounty hunter and wants to remain Anonymous?"

"You know kiddo that just might work, but how do we explain, that spear penetrating through that mans body, we found the other day?"

"Yes, I forgot about that. We could say he fired it out of a harpoon rifle, or something equivalent to that. After seeing how Austenace, fired that thing out of that tube. Not to mention the velocity and accuracy he had with it?"

"I used to wonder how the cave men, could knock down those big Mammoth elephants, and the buffalo back then. Now I understand just how brilliant they were, way back in those cave man days. Maybe we can take some wanted posters back with us, and if Austenaco catches them, or is the reason we catch these people. We can give him the reward money, so he and his people can buy food and other items," John said.

"That sounds like a very good plan John, and before we go out tonight let's run some off on the computer in our office."

"You mean our cubicle, right partner?"

They were both laughing as they pulled into their parking spot, and now they would have to face there biggest challenge of the day, explaining this to Captain Phillips. Just as they entered the big doors, Captain Phillips was waving them into his office.

"Close the door please," He said as they entered.

"Good news Captain, we found an informant, who saw the man who killed that other man in the mountains the other day," John said.

"Did you bring him in? Is he looking through the mug books?

"Not exactly sir, we were able to get a lot of good information from him though. He will be working with us on this case," John said.

"Mister Hammer, are you telling me, that this ordinary citizen is going to help us solve a murder crime. Who dose he, think he is, and what information did he give you?"

"Well Captain. It's a little hard to explain, but here it goes. The man we found today was one of five men who were involved, in the killing of a woman, and her son. When things suddenly went wrong, apparently this man we found dead twisted his ankle slowing him down. So they killed him, not only because he was slowing them down, but to try and shake us off there trail." John said.

"Oh come on John, you expect me to believe this. That spear we pulled out of him was thrown so hard. It went through his body and split his heart in two, now it would have taken someone pounding it in with a sledge hammer, to do that kind of damage. Now you have two choices, either you start telling me the truth, or turn in your shields, because I think you're hiding something from me," Captain Phillips said.

Just as John was going to say something his phone started ringing, he knew who it was by the number. "John here, were a little busy now, can I call you back later."

"If you're not by the train station in ten minutes, there will be another man dead." The phone went dead.

"Captain, before you say anything please come with us fast!" John said.

"What is it John?" Cindy asked.

"That was Austenace, we have to get to the train station in ten minutes, or we will have another body," John said.

Cindy, sat in the back seat with the Captain up in front next to John, and John was weaving in and out of traffic to make the station. When they arrived, Austenace was standing over a man in a blue sports coat. Captain Phillips was unaware of who he was, and he pulled his gun from his holster.

"Freeze son, let the man up," he said.

"No! No! Captain, this is the man we were talking about, he's the one who wants to help us. We made him a deal, that if he saw any of the others, who killed the woman and child, he would contact us. As you can see he's kept his promise," John said.

"Who the hell is he, and who are you to make a deal with anyone, without letting me know first?" Captain Phillips asked.

"You must be the leader of these brave people, you must be real happy with them," Austenace said.

"Who are you mister, and why are you carrying a bow and arrow?" Captain Phillips asked.

"I am called Austenace, but in your language I'd be known as Chief."

"Chief, chief of who?" Captain Phillips asked.

"Well originally of the Paleo's Indians, but now of the Cherokee tribe, I became chief after my father Koatohee passed away. Now I lead my people in the underground world," he said.

"Are you a loony character, what are you talking about, what underground world?" Captain Phillips said.

"Promise me, you will not breathe a word about this, and I will show you. But it must be kept a secret, and the only reason I will show you. Is because you do not believe what my two friends have already told you," Austenace said.

He turned around and started heading farther into a dark hallway, but before they could say anything. They were standing underground once again, and Captain Phillips was now speechless.

"How can this be real? Why? This is impossible, who are you?"

"My people have lived down underground, beneath you for billions of years, and our ancestors hunted and killed the mighty Dinosaur. They lived deep down inside the earth, and learned how to grow plants, flowers, and food. We raised many kinds of animals for feeding, unlike you, and we have plenty of buffalo, and deer to feed our people. We also have walked upon your land, and we see the destruction you've caused. You've chased away the animals by taking away the woods, and building houses. At the rate you're going soon you will run out of food, and have to start killing each other for survival.

I've gone to your schools and learned how to talk your language, I learned how to use your weapons, but I prefer the weapons my ancestors invented. I can go across this country faster than your electric train can, because of the many paths we have underneath the cities. We do not have to stop in certain areas, because of stop signs, or have any speed limits under ground. I've offered to help John and Cindy, because it was my wife and son who were killed. I killed that man they found before, he was one of the men responsible, and unfortunately the other three were able to go free. But they will not be free for long," Austenace said.

"I must say Chief, if I can call you Chief. I'm a little amazed at this discovery, and I understand how important it is to keep it a secret. I will allow you to help John and Cindy, and I hope you find these men who changed your life. But just do me one favor, let at least one of them live, so we can take them to court and put them away for a very long time," Captain Phillips said.

"Thank you Captain, I will do as you ask, but now I have to find this man again, who you let escape. John, I will call you soon," Austenace said. As he lead, them back out into the train station.

When Captain Phillips turned to thank the Chief, he was already gone. "Where did he go so fast?" he asked.

"That's what we've been trying to tell you Captain, he knows the lay of this land better than anyone else I ever knew. He can go from here to there in a heartbeat, and I think he'd be a big asset to our force," John said.

"What are you trying to say Hammer?" Captain asked.

"If I may captain, I put the notion in John's mind, about making Chief Austenace a bounty hunter for our division. Since he can get into places we immediately can't, and find people as fast as he does. We feel he would be a great addition not only to our humane race, but the only problem with this is. He wants to remain anonymous, and doesn't want anyone to know about his underground family," Cindy said.

"That'll be hard for me to do, when I have to make a report to the Mayor and Governor frequently. How can I tell them about the Chief?" he asked.

"You don't have to Captain; you keep this our little secret. Because, just think what could happen. If this world we live in today, found out about Austenace, and the other underground dwellers. It could be a catastrophic turn of events, and it could also be the true meaning of the end of our world," John said.

"I see what you mean John, I just wonder how long this will last before someone else discovers them. Then what, do we hunt them all and kill them too, to protect the world below us?" Captain Phillips asked.

"We can always try it Captain, and if it gets too complicated. We can cut the ties so nobody loses, and we go back to our own way of living," Cindy said.

"Let me think about this on the way back to the precinct, there's just too much to absorb right now. This might even take a couple days to sort out in my mind, and I need to make the right decision here."

"We understand that Captain, but just remember the longer you wait. The more deaths we may encounter if Chief Austenace finds them first," Cindy said.

"That's the hardest part in dealing with this whole thing, to keep his secret, we can't really arrest him. Because then everyone will know who he is, and where he comes from. I hate to think what will happen not only to the underground people, but to humanity itself. Almost every body will be trying to scramble to find gold, or something's of value that is really nothing to them, but of importance to the underground dwellers. It's a lot to put on my plate in today's world, when everyone wants to stick their noses into everything you do today. The more I keep thinking about it, the chief would be a valuable Alai for us," Captain Phillips said.

"That's why you make the big bucks Captain, you make all the right decisions," John said.

"We have to keep this as quiet as possible, from the press."

"What's that Captain?" Cindy asked.

"Staying away from the press, they will eat him up, if they ever found out about Austenaco. Once they get their emotions going, they'll keep snooping around until they find the answer. So it'll be up to you and John, to keep an eye out for the press, and to warn Austenaco about them," Captain Phillips said.

"Only one more question for you sir," said.

"What's on your mind?"

"How are we going to tell the rest of our guy's about Austenaco?"

"We keep quiet about him until the right time."

"When will we know if it's the right time?" Cindy asked.

"As soon as someone else discovers him," Captain Phillips said.

Chapter Eight

As the Captain, John and Cindy entered the precinct doors, they heard a lot of commotion going on between the detectives.

"What's going on in here?" Captain Phillips asked.

"Captain, where have you been? We've been trying to reach you, for the past half hour, and you will not believe what just came over our computers. It seems that someone found an underground city, in Boulder Colorado not only that, they found someone's belongings as if there was actually somebody living down there," Pete Ochoa said.

"What does that have to do with us, here in Racine Wisconsin Pete?" Captain asked.

"Seems like there are trails, underground that spread out all through the United States, and they found footprints that head, toward the north-eastern part of our state," Pete said.

"Pete, why would you think they are here in Wisconsin?" Cindy asked.

"That arrow and spear you two brought in before, ballistics came back a few minutes ago. Seems like the stone that was used on the arrow and spear, was stone called chert, and that hasn't been used since back in the prehistoric days. It so happens that stone was discovered in the underground city, they have just found. Now, if you put two and two together that could spell only one answer. Who ever left that arrow, and threw that spear must have been someone from the underground," Pete said.

"That's a very interesting theory Pete, but what other proof do we have at this time, to put it together?" John asked.

"Nothing conclusive at this time, but it's all we have to go on. So why not go back and check out the area once again, maybe we'll get lucky and find something more concrete," Mary Chaffer said.

"John and Cindy, you go talk to Professor Albert Goodyear,

and see if he's come up with anything else we can use here. Detective's Mary Chaffer and Sam Stone go check with the morgue, and see if they found anything new after doing the other autopsy. Detective's Sidney Sneed, and Pete Ochoa, you two go and check out the murder site, and don't leave ant stone unturned. Maybe we'll get lucky and find something we can finally use. Stay close to your radios in case I need you," Captain Phillips said.

"Everyone scattered like flies looking for somewhere to land, except for John and Cindy. After everyone else left, they turned to Captain Phillips.

"Captain, how in the world, are we supposed to keep this a secret now?" Cindy asked.

"They're only going by suspicion, and a theory that they thought up. After they find out there is no other evidence, to back up what they are thinking, they will give up this non-sense theory of theirs," Captain Phillips said.

"Hopefully they don't find anything, to put it further into their thoughts, or we'll have no choice but to share what we know," John said.

"Why don't you two go talk to Professor Goodyear, and let him in, on what we found. Maybe he'll be able to help out, not only us, but with are new friends down below," Captain said.

"Sounds good Captain, maybe he can squelch some of this talk. I'd hate to be the ones who helped destroy this country, screw up another society of good people," John said.

When John and Cindy made it to where the professor was staying, they went up to his apartment. They found his door broken into, and they withdrew their guns. Slowly they entered the apartment, and saw the room was trashed. As if someone was looking for something, but what would the professor have for anyone. They heard a noise coming from inside the bedroom closet door, as Cindy turned the knob John had his gun ready to fire just in case.

When the latch finally was released, the professor came rolling out, all tied up and gagged. His eyes were the size of silver dollars, and when he saw the detectives he started to smile. After they untied him and took the tape off his mouth.

"I don't know how you knew I was in there, but I do appreciate your help. I thought I was a goner for sure," Professor Goodyear said.

"How long have you been tied up Professor?" Cindy asked.

"I've been in that closet for almost two days," he said.

"Who did this Professor, and what were they after?" John asked.

"It was a couple of big men, one was almost six foot-three, the other was maybe six foot-one. They were looking for the weapons you found on that site this past week, why they didn't say. But since I didn't give them any grief or trouble, they decided to tie me up instead of kill me," he said.

"But if Cindy, and I hadn't come to see you, you might have died, before anyone else would have found you," John said.

"While I was tied up, I had some time to do some serious thinking, and I figured if those weapons fell into the wrong hands. I guess they could make more sophisticated weapons, from the chert stone they had from many years ago, as you saw it wasn't rusty or worn.

"After seeing how tough it was to penetrate right through that mans body, I can understand someone trying to find that kind of stone," John said.

"Mister Hammer, it isn't just the stone, those people don't know how they used those weapons back in those days. Today they have weapons that can hit a target, while they are moving faster than sound. Back then, they had hand held weapons, but they learned how to throw them, and get the velocity to penetrate a Dinosaurs hard skin. Can you imagine how those types of weapons could be used today, with the types of weaponry they have today?" Albert Goodyear asked

"Forget about armor piercing bullets, these would be bone ripping. They'd cut your heart out before you hit the ground," Cindy said.

"Yes, there would be nothing you could wear to avoid getting killed. By the time they'd perfect these bullets, those weapons might be able to penetrate a hard shelled tank," the Professor said.

"Professor, until this is over. I think you should come with us, so we can protect you better. I'll call the Captain and have him set up a place for you to stay, John said.

"That's quite alright mister Hammer, after all they probably think I'm dead by now anyway."

John's phone started to ring, "Hello John here…where are you…we'll be there in five minutes, can I bring someone along to meet you? Yes he's harmless, and could be very beneficial in helping you and your people. Alright we'll see you in five," John said and hung up.

"Professor Goodyear, today must be your lucky day, grab your coat let's go, and I'll introduce you to an old friend," John said.

With Professor Goodyear in the back seat, John headed out toward the hills once again. He was traveling at a high rate of speed, because he knew time was of essence with the Chief. As he entered into the highly secured heavily wooded area, they saw Austenaco standing next to a man, suspended by his ankles from a tree limb.

"Tell me I'm dreaming" the Professor said.

"You're not dreaming professor, now you know why we need to keep, what we found between us," Cindy said.

"Is he for real, can I meet him in person," he asked.

"This is why we asked you to come along Professor Goodyear," John said.

"Hello Austenaco, I take it you found another one of those men who killed your family?" John asked.

"Yes, he is one of the men who raped my wife, before they killed her."

"What were you going to do to him?" John asked.

"I want to make sure he never rapes another woman again."

"How would you do that?" Cindy asked.

"I will cut off his balls, and make him eat them."

"That will stop him alright, but he might die from the blood loss," John said.

"But just think about how much safer others will be, when he is no longer around to cause anymore trouble."

"Can't argue with you there Austenaco, maybe after we're done here you can have your moment with him," John said.

"Hey you can't do that! I have rights," the hanging man said.

"Now, that depends on what you tell us, about your other two friends. What are their names and where can we find them?" John asked.

"I don't know who, or what you're talking about," he said

"He's all yours Austenaco," John said.

"Hey wait, Ok alright I'll tell you, just keep this mad man away from me," he said.

"What's your name?" John asked.

"Billy, Billy Winters, the other who where with me are, Charles White and Jeff Jenkins. But if you kill us, you'll be opening up a big can of whoop ass."

"What are you talking about Billy?" Cindy asked.

"Hey you're a cutie, I'd let you tie me up anytime."

Billy felt a sting in his stomach, as Austenaco hit him with a heavy closed fist. Blood trickled out of Billy's mouth, and John knew the force of his fist, must have broken something inside his stomach.

"Billy, unless you want to feel more pain, just answer the questions. Who else are you working with?" John asked.

"It's a whole network of people, and we're spread out all across the United States. We take care of each other, and if you kill us they will put you on the extinction list. It doesn't matter who you are, or what you do, they will find you, and kill you," Billy said.

"Who is the man in charge?" Cindy asked.

"There isn't only one man in charge," Billy said.

"Bull Billy, there is always only one man to report too. Now what is his name?" John asked.

"I report to a man named Nick Austin, I don't know if he's the main man. But that's all I have for you," Billy said.

"Where can I find him?" John asked.

"If you kill me, you will not have to find him, because he will find you."

"Then what are we wasting our time for here, Austenaco do your thing,"

"Wait! Wait! Wait! Alright I'll tell you, just make the pain stop please," Billy pleaded.

"Alright Billy, you tell us the truth without any BS this time, and we'll relieve the pain in your legs," John said.

"Alright he calls us from Boulder City I don't know where he lives. I only talk to him over the phone," Billy said.

"You said there are others living here, where are they?" Cindy asked.

"They're spread all over the city, and you will not even see them coming until it's too late. Before you know, where they are, you'll be dead," Billy said.

"Since you have no more information for us, you're no good to us anymore. Normally we would take you back to prison with us, but since you're responsible for killing Austenaco's family, I think justice should be up to him. What do you think Billy?"

"Are you kidding me, she was a dirty squaw, and a bony little kid. They were nothing but scum, and they deserved to die," Billy said.

John and Cindy turned there backs on Billy, and asked the Professor what he thought.

"Since Billy has no remorse for taking Austenaco's family

away from him, I think Austenaco should be able to choose Billy's fate," Professor Goodyear said.

"We totally agree with you Professor, and so it'll be. Austenaco, we will leave you to take care of Billy as you please. But we will need your help getting the others too, can we count on you?" John asked.

"Because, of what they did to my family, I will help you, until every one of them meet their own fate. I know how to get in touch with you, and there are still two more out there I have to get yet. I thank you for letting me have justice today, and I'm forever indebted to be your friend, and help you in anyway I can. I will call you soon," Austenaco said.

"Hey you can't leave me with this behemoth; he'll cut me in half. I told you everything I know, you said you would let me go," Billy yelled.

John turned around. "Billy, I never said I'd let you go, I said I'd ease your pain. Now you play good with your new friend, and maybe we'll see each other in another world. Hope your day is a slice," John said as they walked away, leaving Austenaco, and Billy alone. When they turned around to wave goodbye, they were both gone from sight. Billy will get a bird's eye view of their underground city, and now they had a couple more names to look up when they get back to the office.

Professor Goodyear decided to stay with John and Cindy after meeting Austenaco. He understood how important, it was to keep it a secret to the rest of the world. He was also worried, about what would happen if the rest of the world ever found out, but on the other hand, he wondered if what was happening now, was in Gods plan to try and save this world.

Chapter Nine

Captain Phillips was waiting for John and Cindy back in his office, and when they came through the door with Professor Goodyear, he looked a little confused. Curios about who the older gentleman was as the captain approached with caution.

"Hello John, Cindy who's your guest?" he asked.

"Captain Phillips, this is Professor Albert Goodyear, he's the archeologist who's working with us on the Austenaco case," Cindy said.

After shaking hands, "Welcome to our precinct Professor, have you come up with anything here that makes sense?" Captain Phillips asked.

"Please Captain, call me Albert. Yes I've been surprised at what I've discovered since I've been here, and now I have had the opportunity to actually meet Austenace. I can't believe that this isn't a dream, and when I wake up, I'll be at home in my own bed. But since I can feel the change in the air temperature, I know this isn't a dream. Is it really possible, for these people to actually be living right underneath us? I need to find out more about Austenaco and his people," Professor said.

"We're just as confused as you are Albert, but we're working diligently to find out just what is going on," Captain Phillips said.

"How did you find Austenace?" the Professor asked.

"We didn't actually find him, he is the one who found us," John said. Then he proceeded to tell the Professor the whole story.

While John explained the events up to this point, Austenaco was about to get busy, with another one of the men he was after. He had a wide smile on his face, when he saw it was the one, who got away from him earlier today at the bus terminal.

Walking into the tavern, he approached the bar and ordered a draft beer. He was acting like he was reading the newspaper, until he was interrupted by the bar tender.

"Hey buddy you must be new around here, my name is Charlie, and this is my establishment. I've never seen you before, are you new to this area?"

"Yes I guess you can say that, this is a very nice place you have here Charlie. I'll have to visit it more often, but first I have a little unfinished business I must do. Have you seen this man anywhere?" Austenaco said, and handed him a picture.

After shaking hands, Charlie said. "Yes I've seen him, and in fact, I believe it's the man in the back shooting pool. He's not in any trouble is he?"

"That depends on if he wants to make any trouble Charlie, if anything happens call this number. Ask for Detective John Hammer, and let him know what's going on. In fact maybe you might want to call him now," Austenaco said.

As Charlie started to dial he heard the big stranger say.

"Hey Billy, do you remember me from earlier today?"

"You stay away from me man, or I'll be sending you to meet your wife and kid," he said.

Austenaco moved very quick grabbing Billy by the throat and with one arm, pulled him forward, and now they were face to face. He didn't see the other man coming up from behind him, but he saw Billy's eyes grow wide, and he turned around without releasing his grip on Billy. The bar stool came crashing down upon Billy's head instead of Austenacos. With one punch he sent Billy sailing against the back wall, and then turned his attention to the other man in front of him. He was still holding the chair in his hands, and as he tried to swing it again. Austenaco grabbed his forearm, and twisted his arm around, and with a vicious hammer strike to his elbow. He hit him with so much force, he left the man with his arm dangling free of his elbow. He heard the noise of footsteps coming form behind him. Quickly Austenaco turned and with a powerful straight arm, he hit the other man square in the nose, with his bug ham hock open hand, Charlie thought he broke the mans neck, as his neck snapped back fast, and he fell to the floor. Austenaco sat back down at the bar, and then asked.

"Charlie, did you call that number, I asked you too?"

"Yes, Austenaco I did, and may I say. That was an impressive show you just put on, remind me never to make you mad at me," Charlie said.

"He was one of the five men who killed my wife and son, and he's the second one I've sent to the grave. I still have two more to find, but I will stay here until my friends show up. I never run from a fight, and if they don't believe what I say, then I could be justly accused of my wrong doings," Austenaco said.

"Austenaco, you were just defending yourself, everyone saw them attack you first. Just tell them you feared for your life," Charlie said.

John and Cindy were driving like a mad bull going after a matador, trying to get to the bar before anyone else, and help Austenaco. This was one thing they thought he could never handle on his own, and when they finally arrived seeing everything as quiet as can be. They both entered the bar, and saw Austenaco sitting at the bar, with his new found friends laughing.

"John and Cindy, it's about time you made it here. There are three goons tied up in the back pool room, don't worry they aren't going anywhere," Austenaco said.

"Austenaco, you scared us out of our wits. We were thinking you were in trouble here, and we almost hit a few cars on the way. Now we find you sitting around the bar, talking and laughing. Please explain this to us," John said.

"I found out that the guy I caught before at the train station, had been seen in this tavern. I thought I'd come and check it out, and then I'd catch him again, before I called you.

But he had other idea's about trying to run again, and he had help from a couple other guys," Austenaco said.

When they walked into the back room of the bar, John and Cindy saw the three men laid out flat as pancakes. They went over to try and revive them, but when nobody moved. John was afraid maybe Austenaco killed them, until he heard a grunt come out of one of the guys.

"How long ago did you take these men out?" Cindy asked.

"Maybe a half hour before you walked through the door," Austenaco said.

"Austenaco, if you're living in the hills, how did you get here? When there are no hills around this area for miles?" John asked.

"We have many tunnel entrances and exits underground, everything is not how it looks. We are able go anywhere we want, without any interference with traffic lights. By the way the man I killed before, apparently had some money someone was looking for, and now they think the two of you have taken it. They will not stop until they either have the money back, or the two of you are dead," Austenaco said.

"Who was the guy? Did you get a name? What did he look like?" John asked.

"He's a big man, not on height only standing 5'10" but he was very strong looking. Light brown skin, and liked to smoke little tiny brown cigarettes," Austenace said.

"That sounds like Alvin Ruiz, he's one of the biggest mobsters here in Racine, and the only rules he follows are his own.

"If you know who he is, go and get him," Austenaco said.

"Believe me, Austenace; there is nothing more I'd like do than, put that guy away for a long time. But we have rules, we have to live by in our world," Cindy said.

"That is the one thing, I find very wrong in your world. Why do you cater to the people who do others wrong, and hurt the innocent people? Especially those who run from you, and don't fess up to their crime," Austenaco asked.

"I wish I had the answer for you my friend, but unfortunately there are some who think that even the guilty, have more rights than those who have never committed a crime. Not only that this society as it is now, is slowly stripping away our constitutional rights. My fear is that our great nation might crumble, from the inside, without having to go to war. We need to straighten out our own backyard, and stop worrying about so many others around the nation," John said.

"That is the one thing I do not understand, about the people who lead you. I understand, the reason for helping others, but I think that first you must fix your own problems. That is what made you the strongest nation before?" Austenaco asked.

"I've been asking that same question for years Austenace, why is it we can see and help the people starving in other countries, but we are blind to the ones starving in our own backyard. Just drive around the White House, and see all the people sitting around the fence looking for food and jobs. I think our leaders have blinders on, when it comes to seeing, and helping those they have sworn to lead," John said.

"If they would do as they promise, by bringing in good paying jobs. For those who want to work, so they can once again have pride in feeding their families. I don't mind helping those who are trying to make it, or the ones who can't work due to illness or injuries. By bring back jobs, instead of leaning on the ones who are trying to make a living working already, sooner or later even the ones who are working, will also be on the bread line. You can't keep taking away from those who have, and give it to those who have not. Unless you want more people losing their houses, due to having so much money taken out of their checks, that they can't make the payments anymore," Cindy said.

"We have no problems, with people starving in our village, and there is always plenty for all to eat. We even have places for them to sleep, if they have no place to go. We believe, like you did at one time, we should help our neighbor," Austenace said.

"What about those who break the laws in your village?" Cindy asked.

"We have no laws, only honor system, and if someone breaks

that, they are cast off to live all alone. They will either live a long lonely life, or end up being eaten by the animals of the forests," Austenaco said.

"Then you have someone from our world, which discovers a way to enter your world, and takes your most beloved belongings. Your wife and son, and what happens after you find all of those responsible?" John asked.

"Then I will go and grieve the death of my family in my own world," Austenaco said.

"How do you get money to help pay for your seeds, and other items you need?" Cindy asked.

"Sometimes it is difficult and I must travel into your world, and work for a short while to make enough money, to pay for the seeds and grain needed," Austenaco said.

John called Captain Phillips, and wanted to know what to do about Austenaco. If they bring him in, everyone would know about who he is, and they didn't want any more trouble to brew up.

"John send me a picture of the three men the big Chief just captured, let me do some digging on this end," he said. Then he waited as John sent the pictures from his Smart Phone as requested to the Captain, and then he waited by his phone. Within minutes the Captain was back on the phone.

"John, let the Chief go," he said.

"Sorry Captain, could you please repeat what you had just said?" John asked.

"Let the Chief go, it seems like all three of the victims had bounties on their heads. In fact, we own the Chief a little over thirty-thousand dollars, for the capture of the pool gang," Captain said.

"Say that again Captain, so I know I heard you right?" John asked.

"Billy Winters, Charles White and Jeff Jenkins are known as the pool bandits, they spend all night shooting pool at the bar. They stay until the last person leaves, and then rob the place. They very seldom leave witnesses, in fact the only reason we have knowledge about them now. Is because one of their victims faked his death, and they never check him, before they left the bar. Not only did he give us good descriptions, he had the video tapes to show how they operated the theft. These warrants just came out a couple weeks ago," Captain Phillips said.

"Austenaco, are these the other three men who killed your family?" John asked.

"Only the one whose neck I broke, the other two I never saw before."

"Captain, looks like we are not finished here yet, Austenaco says, only Billy Winters is who he was after, the other two he never saw before. But the good news is we're halfway to ending this nightmare for Austenace," John said.

"You're a trip Hammer, now release the Chief, and get back to the precinct. After they haul the bodies out of the bar of course, say hello to the Chief," Captain Phillips said.

"Did I do something wrong John?" Austenaco asked.

"No in fact, you stopped a possible theft and murder attempt my friend. Captain Phillips told me, you have money coming to you for capturing them," John said.

"What do you mean, by money coming, John."

"These men have warrants out on them, and apparently, they've done this many times before. They've always been successful, that is until they ran into you. You have money coming to you," John said.

"We could certainly use a few things in our village, how much money do you think I will get John?"

"Captain Phillips wasn't really sure, but he said, he thinks somewhere around thirty-thousand dollars," John said.

"Why will they pay, that much money for these men?"

"Not all bounties are this much Austenaco, it depends on what they did, and who wants them. It could be as little as two-hundred dollars, or as much as a million, depending on the risk it might take to capture these people. The crimes could range from bail jumping, to murder, such as this one here. I know you can't come in and get the money, and so I'll deliver it to you when it arrives," John said.

"Thank you John, and even though I don't understand why they would pay me, to capture or kill the ones who do wrong. I can always use the money, to buy food and medicine for my people, I will see you soon my friend."

"I will contact you when the payment comes in, and in the mean time I'll be waiting for your next call. Stay safe my friend," John said.

Chapter Ten

After the scene was all cleaned up, and the prisoners were loaded into the paddy wagon, everyone said their goodbyes. John and Cindy were speeding back to the precinct, when a call came over their radio.

"Hammer, we just received a call from another officer. It looks like he stumbled onto a robbery in progress, at the Chase bank on Wisconsin Avenue. He said it's a hostage situation the negotiators are on their way. Keep everything in check, until they arrive, we have Pete Ochoa, and Mary Chauffer on their way to back you up," the dispatcher said.

"Nothing like making our day a little more interesting hey partner," Cindy said.

"Relax Cindy, this is why they pay us the big bucks," John said.

"I just hope they don't lose it before we get there, and start shooting people," Cindy said.

"Me too, I think we've seen enough killing in one day already. Maybe Austenaco knows another way in that bank," John said.

"John, why should Austenaco, get involved with this? If he wants to stay out of the newspaper, why would he want to help us now?

"I guess your right, but I'll let him know if he needs us, we might be a little tied up."

John dialed his old phone, and on the third ring Austenaco answered a bit reluctantly.

"Hello," he said.

"Austenaco, John here, I hate to bother you now my friend. Cindy and I will be busy for awhile, and so if you need us, it might be a little difficult to get a hold of us," John said.

"Do you want my help?"

"Thanks Austenaco, but it could get awful bright around here real soon. And if you want to stay in the shadows, it's probably best better you stay away. I just wanted to let you know that if you need us later tonight, we could be tied up," John said.

"John, do me a favor, keep your phone on, and don't hang up," Austenaco said.

"What's the reason for that?" John asked.

"So I know what's going on, and in case you need my help. Where are you?" Austenaco asked.

"We're just pulling up now, at the Chase bank on Wisconsin Avenue, and everything looks alright. Wait no I just saw a flash in the doorway, that tint on those doors is a little dark I think. If not for the sun's rays, I wouldn't have seen the flash of light, and now here comes our negotiating team. I have to put you on hold my friend, but I will not hang up," John said.

John stuck his phone in his top shirt pocket, as he walked over to the parked car. When the man stepped out of his door, he asked.

"Are you the officer who called this in?" he asked.

That's when it finally dawned on John and Cindy, where the guy who called this in was.

"John, look over in the far corner," Cindy said. They saw a downed officer struggling to get up.

John looked over and saw Pete and Mary, pull up in their car, he motioned for them to back him up, and he ran toward the downed officer. But when he made it over to him, the man was holding a gun on John.

"Don't make a foolish move officer, and you might live to see tomorrow. Let's go inside the bank shall we," he said.

Cindy's heart fell down to her knees, as she watched John heading into the bank, with a gun pressed against his back. She was a little surprised when John looked into her direction and smiled, it was as almost he expected to be led into the bank. Cindy had to shake her head clear, as thoughts of John being involved with these bank robbers crossed her mind.

Cindy wasn't sure, if John planned to be taken inside, or things just went wrong. Then she noticed the man holding the gun into John's back, was an old collar they had back when she just started her detective job. He must have recognized John and decided to try and strengthen his position in the negotiating process. Cindy heard her name, and when she turned Mary Chauffer was signaling her over to them. When Cindy was by her side, Mary handed Cindy her phone.

"Hello," she said.

"Cindy, this is Captain Phillips, what in thunder nation is going on over there. I was just informed that Hammer was just taken as a hostage, what was he thinking?" he asked.

"John was just trying to help out a downed officer, and stake the place out to see if there was anyway we could surround the area. Hank Simmons had another idea," Cindy said.

"What the hell is he doing there? Why did I have to hear it on the police radio?" Captain Phillips asked.

"Don't know for sure Captain, but he's the one who was holding the gun to John's back, as they walked him into the bank," Cindy said.

"What is he doing out of prison? Are you sure it was him? Let…" Captain was interrupted.

"Hold on Captain, the front door of the bank just opened up, and six women and three children were sent out. Maybe John gave himself up to save those people," Cindy said.

"Now, that I believe John would do, but don't you think of doing anything that foolish. I have enough on my plate to worry about, without having to worry about my Detectives too. I'm finishing up some paper work, and then I'll be heading over there, just don't do anything to justify getting hurt. Keep your phone close, and call me if anything else develops before I get there. Tell Mary and Pete, to watch there backs and yours," Captain Phillips said and then hung up.

"Captain, heard about John being taken, he said he heard it on the radio. He'll be here in a few minutes I don't know what he's going to do," Cindy said.

"Well John and the Captain go back a long way Cindy, in fact John saved his life a couple times, when they were beat cops. I guess the Captain thinks, he owes John to be here," Pete said.

"What the hell was John thinking… pulling a stunt like that?" Cindy asked.

"You just saw the answer to that, when those women and children were released," Mary said.

"Cindy, don't worry, after knowing and working with John these past few years, I can tell you this much. John didn't do that, without having a back up plan to get out," Pete said.

"Yes, I've seen him do some incredible things myself, but I just can't keep thinking that one of these times, it just might back fire on him," Pete said.

"Why don't you try calling him on his cell phone?" Mary asked.

Cindy tried, and only received a busy signal, at first she couldn't figure it out. Until she remembered John's last phone call to Austenaco, and then a smile formed on her face. This was John's plan, and now they'd have to wait and see, when Austenaco would show up.

Captain Phillips pulled up, within fifteen minutes after talking to Cindy, and he walked over to Mary and Pete. Then he went to talk to Cindy.

"Anything new I should know about agent Sharp?" he asked.

"Only that John's phone is still on."

"Now what is that supposed to mean?" he asked.

"Unless I'm wrong Captain, which I doubt in this case I am. I think Austenaco is on the other end of that phone connection, and if anyone could find a way into that bank, like he did back at that tavern a little while ago. I think John and everyone else inside will be safely

64

returned," Cindy said.

"I hope your right my dear, because if not, many good people could die tonight," Captain Phillips said.

"I've worked with negotiator Rick King before sir, and he's good at talking people out of situations like this," Mary said.

"He's a very good talker, but the problem isn't him. It's Hank Simmons, and he's a two time felon with six murders on his records. He was scheduled to go to the gas chamber in Texas next year, for killing a bank clerk there. We were holding him here, while they were sending someone to pick him up, and somehow he was released from prison. If there's anyone who doesn't care about dying it's him," Captain Phillips said.

"If we can hang on long enough, I think we'll have the element of surprise Captain," Cindy said.

"Why's that?" he asked.

"Austenaco," she said.

"If you don't mind my asking Captain, who's this Austenaco guy, you two keep talking about?" Pete asked.

"Just a good friend, we met a few days ago, he has ways of getting into places we could never get into. He's kind of like a today's Houdini," Captain Phillips said.

Negotiator Rick King finally had a response from a phone call.

"Hello this is negotiator Rick King, let's talk about your situation here ok?" he asked.

"No it is I, who will begin this conversation, I want five million dollars, and a helicopter here within two hours or I start killing people. There are twenty-five hostages in here, and I suggest you get about six pizzas delivered her, and if they should happen to die because of you, they might as well die on a full stomach," he said.

"I'll try to meet your request, but first I have to see a sign of good faith. Send out John Hammer, as I dial for your pizzas" Rick said.

"If I don't see the pizza here in half an hour, I'll send him out to you. But it'll be in a body bag," Hank said.

Cindy was calculating the possibilities of getting John, and the others out of there. She was looking at the map of the bank, when she saw a flash of light from the corner of her eye. Thinking it was probably a reflection of the sun in a window, she went back to the map. But then it dawned on her, it was almost three o'clock in the afternoon, there was no sun out in the east now, and her shadow was now playing peek-a-boo with the ground. Then another crazy idea popped into her head, *'Is it possible, could it be Austenaco, and he really understood, John was in trouble? How was he going to get into the bank, without triggering off the alarm?"* Cindy came back to reality, and decided all she had was wishful thinking. Just to be on the safe side, she thought she'd go and check it out. Even if it's nothing, at least she'd have a clearer head not thinking about it so much.

"Hey Officer Sharp, where do you think you're going?" Captain Phillips asked.

"Just thought I saw something Captain, thought I'd go check it out," she said.

Captain Phillips was about to say something, before Cindy gave him a wink. Then it finally dawned on him, that maybe they had another Alai on their side. But how was the Chief, going to help them now? Captain Phillips thought.

Cindy, made it to where she figured the flash appeared, and there in the mud next to the door. She saw a footprint by the back window, and it was the same size as the other they found by the rocks. However, this one wasn't bare footed, but looking closer, she could swear it was a moccasin imprint. *"If this was indeed Austenace, then where did the other footprint go? There was no sign of the window being forced open, and she knew he couldn't have just walked through the window.'* She thought to herself, and then as she looked around a little longer. She saw another half print going into the wall, and when she pressed her hand against it. She found herself standing inside the basement of the bank. Then she heard something that startled her.

"Cindy, I was wondering, how long it would take you to find my secret pathway."

"Austenaco, how did you manage to get through the wall?" Cindy asked.

"I'll explain it to you later, but first we have to save John and the others inside the bank. Are you ready to rescue these people?" Austenaco asked.

"Yes I'm ready Austenaco, what is your plan?" Cindy asked.

"I'm going to try and draw a few guys down here, and then we'll capture them and hopefully have some idea of what we got ourselves into," Austenaco said.

"By coincidence, just how in the world are you going to get them down here, without them shooting us first?" she asked.

"Because, they will not be able to see us right away, we'll blend in with our surroundings."

Cindy was trying to figure out what Austenaco had in mind, until he led her to the stairway. He slid her underneath the stairs, but with plenty of light to see in front of her. Then he took some white powder, and coated his skin with it. When he curled against the wall, it was like magic. As he seemed to disappear before her eyes, Austenaco was a big Indian, and it seemed almost impossible for him to do this.

Austenaco took out his war club and struck the water pipe, the sound echoed through the basement. Soon the door opened up, and down the stairs came three men holding automatic weapons.

"Jerry! I thought you checked this whole place out before," Kevin said.

"Relax Kevin, it was probably just some air in the water pipes," Jerry said.

"But we have to make the boss happy, so let's check it out anyway," Roger said.

"Don't tell me that, Mister Body builder is scared of a little noise?" Kevin asked.

Just as Kevin had finished his question, Austenaco stuck a big hunting knife straight through his kidney. Jerry was startled and started reaching for his weapon, and Cindy came out form underneath the stairway. She hit Jerry in the back of his head hard, with the butt of her gun, knocking him out. Roger just froze in his tracks when he saw the big Indian looking at him.

"How many people are there, in your party?" Cindy asked.

He didn't answer at first, but when Austenaco made a move toward him. "Twelve total, there are twelve," he said.

"How many, have weapons and what kind?"

"Four have automatic rifles, two have .12 barrel shotguns, and the rest have automatic hand guns," Roger said.

"How many prisoners are up there?"

"Last count we made, I believe there was thirty-two counting that stupid cop we caught before," he said.

"Well it's because of that stupid cop being caught, we're here. You see he has a hidden camera in his coat, and because of our little set up. We know exactly if you're telling the truth, and so far Roger, you're doing good. Now one last question before we lock you up down here. What's the name of your leader in this job?" Cindy asked.

"I've only heard someone call him Hank, and that's all I know honest. You're not gong to kill me are you?" Roger asked.

"No Roger I will not kill you, but if what you tell me isn't true. I will send Austenaco back down here, and have him torture you, before you die," Cindy said.

Roger saw the big Indian looking at him, and his eyes seemed to say, he was going to enjoy torturing him. Sweat started to form around Roger's head, and he knew the shoe was now on the other foot. He also knew that sooner or later, they would miss him upstairs and come down to find him. He just had to make sure that, he stayed alive long enough to be rescued. Roger was wondering how this detective was going to surprise the others upstairs, as far as he knew there was only one way up, and that was the way he came down.

Austenaco, walked over to Roger, and pulled out a long scarf from his pocket. He balled up the middle of the scarf rolling it into a ball, and he then inserted it into Roger's mouth. Before Roger could say anything, not only was he gagged, but a hood was put over his head. It was only a short time, before the hood was taken off his head. When he finally had his sight back, he noticed the girl was gone, and he was now alone with the giant Indian.

Chapter Eleven

Cindy wasn't exactly sure, where this underground tunnel would take her. But she had this growing confidence, that Austenaco was there to help them, and if she followed his instructions. She new they would prevail, and then she came to the end of her trail. Cindy found the rock she had to move, and when she moved it to the right. The wall seemed to open up easily, but only she could see it move. Slowly she stepped out, and found herself standing in a room right behind the other thieves. When she looked to the right of her, she saw John, tied up in the corner. She crouched down, and gracefully moved over by John, and when she had him free. Cindy handed him her spare gun, she kept her finger on her lips.

Slowly, they moved back to the hidden opening, and Cindy pushed John back into the tunnel. John was a bit startled at first, to see Cindy here, but when he saw Austenaco as they re-entered his world. He saw the two dead men lying on the ground, and the third tied up and gagged.

"Austenaco, I should have known it was you, but how did you know, I was in trouble?" John asked.

"This little device here, I talked to you on, I told you not to shut it off, in case you needed me, and then you sent me something else, I don't know what it was," Austenaco said.

"I sent you a picture of the man, who's in charge in this bank robbery, and I thought maybe you could send it to Captain Phillips. Here let me show you, how to use it," John said.

When the picture came into view, John thought Austenaco, was about to lose his cool.

"What's wrong Austenaco?" Cindy asked.

"He's one of the men who killed my family, and now he must pay the ultimate price. He must die," Austenaco said.

"Hold it Austenaco, I want this man bad too, but we can't

chance getting those other innocent people killed. We have to figure out a way to save them, before we go charging in there," John said.

"Austenaco, are there any other ways to get into that bank, without them knowing it?" Cindy asked.

"Yes…but if we bring them back into my world, our secret will be lost forever."

"What if we could guarantee you that wouldn't happen?" John asked.

"What do you have in mind John?" Cindy asked.

"Austenaco, how many ways can we get into this bank from here?" John asked.

"Before this building was here, there were many ways, to exit into your world. But now that this building is here, some of our exits have been closed up. But there could still be four other ways they haven't blocked. I was fortunate about the one I found by you, was open, and now I know where the others should be," Austenaco said.

"Good… if we go in three different ways hopefully, we can get those innocent people to safety. Then we can concentrate, on getting those scum bags out of there," John said.

"I have heard this word used many times, what are scum bags?" Austenaco asked.

"They are people who like to hurt others," John said.

"Scumbags…I like that," Austenaco said. 'Let's go I'll show you the way in."

Cindy, and John, followed Austenaco down a dark path. If not for the little candles burning on the walls, they wouldn't even see each other. They were both wondering where they were, first they were in daylight, and as quick as a wink, they were in the dark. What seemed like forever only took a couple minutes. Austenaco motioned for them to stop, and when they did.

"Don't move from here, I'll be right back," he said.

Before they could say anything, he was gone, and they were now alone together in the dark.

"This is a bit creepy isn't it?" Cindy asked.

"I don't know, just think about, what we could do now, without getting caught," John said.

"Just like a man, to think of sex at a time like this."

"Hey baby, if not for sex, we wouldn't be here now," John said laughing.

Cindy, was about to say something, but then Austenaco came back into sight.

"I found two another ways into this building, one way is behind a big counter. The other is almost off to the right, and is in plan sight. If they don't see you exit, you'll need two steps without being seen, until you get behind the counter," Austenaco said.

"Ok, since I'm a little bit more light footed, I'll take the open way in and pray," John said. Cindy, can take the one behind the counter, and what about you Austenaco. Which way will you be going in?" John asked.

"The ways you are going in, you will find the people you look for, after you help them. I will circle around, and come in the other way, and you will wait five minutes. Then I will draw their attention to me, so you can shoot them without any problems."

"Austenaco, are you telling us, we should shoot them in the back? I don't think I can do that," John said.

"Then, you distract them, and I will kill them from behind," he said.

"Austenaco, it's against my personal judgment, not to shoot anyone in the back. I just can't bring myself to doing something like that, I'm sorry," John said.

"Do you know how my wife died?" Austenaco asked.

"I figured she died while they were raping her," John said.

"That was only part of it, after they were done. They gave my son to her, and as she hugged my boy's head close to hers. They put the gun barrel directly to the back of her head, and the bullet went through both of their heads. I seek the justice, that my world would put them through," Austenaco said.

John couldn't believe what he was hearing, and he held back a few tears that surfaced in his eyes. He patted Austenaco on the back. "My friend, we will do it your way I hope, that their time comes soon, for them to meet their true maker. I will shoot them in the back, as a favor to you," John said.

Without saying another word Austenaco was gone, and both John and Cindy knew it wouldn't take him long to get to his destination. They departed for there own entrances, as they were instructed to do. Only problem was when they made it to where they were supposed to be, nothing was marked. They had to feel around until they found the secret entrance, and when Cindy pushed on her door. She thought she'd have to push hard, but to her surprise. She found herself falling through the opening, and rolling onto the floor. She felt embarrassed, but what the heck, nobody was even there to see her fall in.

John found his entrance, and was getting ready to sneak into the bank, he took a heavy breathe. He started to push the panel out, and then he heard the phone start ringing. Remembering, where the phone was, he knew he had a golden opportunity, to exit without being seen.

As he made it through, he scooted in behind the counter, and sat down. Then he heard a little of the conversation from the phone call.

"Hey, you said, you'd have that chopper here in half an hour, and your time is almost up. If we don't hear that chopper in the next fifteen minutes, we start eliminating people. I think we'll start with that stupid cop, who we caught before," he was laughing as he hung up the phone.

"Hey Fred, where's Roger, Kevin and Jerry they should have been back up here, a while ago. You better go check on them, they better not be playing around, or I'll kill them," Hank said. "Carl, bring that pretty boy cop over here will you?"

"Hey Hank, I thought you said, he was behind this counter?" Carl asked.

"Stop messing with my head Carl, that isn't very nice," Hank said.

"I'm serious boss, he's gone, not a trace of him around anywhere,' Carl said.

Hank walked over to look for him, and when he discovered John was gone. He became angry, and started to throw things around. "How could he have gotten away? With the way he was tied up, he can't be far, spread out and make sure he isn't hiding anywhere. If he's not found by the time we need him, we'll just have to eliminate someone else when the time is up," Hank said.

John was hoping Austenaco gave the signal fast, or they might find him before they could make a move. John wasn't surprised to hear the next problem that popped up on Hank.

"Hey boss, Kevin, and Jerry are dead, and I didn't see anything of Roger. It's like he disappeared," Fred said.

"What do you mean disappeared? How could he have left without us seeing him?" Hank asked. "What the hell is going on here today, we lose the cop and now Roger."

"I don't know what's going on here boss, but how can he vanish into thin air, and without a trace?" Fred said.

"Roger isn't the only one missing, that detective is missing too. What on earth is going on here?" Hank asked.

Just as Hank finished his question, Fred slapped his neck. Before he could say anything, he folded up like an accordion, and fell to the floor.

"Come on Fred stop playing games, there's enough freaky things happening today," Hank said.

Carl went over to shake Fred, and then he backed off fast with a stunned look on his face. "He's dead!"

"What do you mean he's dead, we were just talking a split second ago, he can't be dead," Hank said.

Connie Freeman went over to check on Fred, and when she

confirmed, that he was indeed dead. "What kind of stuff, have you got me into here Hank? I was only supposed to help you get in, and out of here. It was only going to be a thirty second job you said, and now, I'm in the middle of a hostage situation. Now you have some kind of Voodoo thing happening here. How are you going to get out of this jamb?" she asked.

"Well Connie, I wasn't expecting company this soon outside. Someone from inside this bank must have pushed the silent alarm button. Now we have to play the waiting game," Hank said.

"Game, you think this is a game you're playing here Hank, more people could die before this is over. I don't want to play this game with you anymore, I want out Hank," Connie said.

"You want out Connie, you're wish will be granted. Since we don't have our detective to execute, you've just volunteered to be the first victim. Then you'll be free once again," Hank said.

Connie looked sick to her stomach, and she thought Hank would just let her go. Now she saw the true side of Hank, he was a cold hearted killer. He didn't care for anybody else but himself and now, she had sealed her own fate.

"Hey Hank, you shouldn't have upset that young lady," John said.

"Hello John, I knew you were still here. Keep talking we'll find you," Hank said.

"Hank, drop your weapons and put your hands over your heads. You're surrounded, and there is no escape, you have fifteen seconds to make up your mind."

"I don't know, how you killed those other men, but you will pay for that. Why don't you show yourself, and Carl or Jason will bring you back here to me," Hank said.

John stood straight up, from behind the counter. "I tried to warn you, but I didn't think you were that smart. If you or anyone, from your goon squad makes any move toward me, you'll never make another move again."

Carl, grinned and took a step toward John, and as soon as he put his foot down. There was a whistle, and a stream of air blew by Hanks ear. Before he knew what happened, Carl was lying flat on his stomach, with a big arrow sticking through his neck.

"What on earth is going on here? Where did that arrow come from?" Hank asked.

"Hank, think back in your sick mind, do you remember, that little Indian woman and her son, you killed a few days ago?" John said.

"How could you know about that, there's no way, anyone could have found that out. We stumbled on an opening, in the rocks by mistake, and before we could exit. We were discovered by that woman, and her son. I had to do something, so she wouldn't talk," Hank said.

"So instead of just leaving, you decided to rape her, and kill them both. That wasn't to smart Hank, because you angered her people. They've sworn to get revenge, and their day of reckoning is here. But, there's still two more of you left, who's the remaining members of your party who you were with?" John asked.

"Are you for real, there's no way you could arrest me for anything that happened, there are no witnesses," Hank said.

"But there was a witness, and in fact he's killed two of you already, when you were running away. I believe it was Nick Austin, and then he caught up with Billy Winters earlier today, and now he's here to settle the score with you," John said.

"You're math is wrong John, there were only four of us," Hank said.

"Four of you, who actually rapped and killed that woman and the little boy, but you had a driver, and if my math is correct that would make five. Am I right Hank?"

"If you have a witness, where is he?"

"Standing right behind you Hank," John said.

As Hank turned around, John said. "Hank this is Austenaco, he's the husband of the woman and child you killed. He's also the Chief of his tribe, and he has some business to take care of with you."

"If I tell you the other two men's names, will you let me go?" Hank pleaded.

"Depends on what you tell me first Hank," John said.

"The other guy who helped rape the woman is Ron Saxony, and the driver was Phil Rush. Ron stays on the north side of town, and Phil could be anywhere. He likes to travel a lot normally, he hits the sports bars."

"Thanks Hank, now if you would drop your weapons, and raise your hands," John said.

When they didn't respond to the last request, shots erupted, and all the bad guys lay dead on the floor, except for Hank, he was left standing. Hank thought he was in the clear, until Austenaco approached him.

"Hey, you said we had a deal John," Hank said.

"We do Hank I said I wouldn't hurt you. However, you should have asked Austenaco. I don't think he would have granted it Hank, because there is only one thing on his mind, and that's getting his revenge for your crime, Austenaco, have fun with your new playmate."

Austenaco, hit Hank with a hard right hand, and as he folded up in his arms. He picked Hank up like he was a rag doll, slung him over his shoulder and started walking away.

"Where are you going Austenaco?" Cindy asked.

"I will take this man back to my village, where we will make him suffer, many times before we kill him. He's one of the three, who took my wife, before they killed my family. Now he shall find out, what the punishment is for taking a life, in our world. But today, he'll walk through hell, before he meets his other world," Austenaco said.

As the front door opened up and the reporters and their TV crews rushed in, John looked around and Austenaco was gone. He shuttered as he thought in his own mind, what Hank is about to go through. John remembered reading an article he found, back when he was surfing the internet, after they first met Austenaco. Some of those men they tortured, back in their time, they would peel back the bottom skin of their feet. Then they would have the women sew the skin back, after adding corn or little pebbles inside their skin, and force them to run around the camp. Some were in so much pain, that they would jump off cliffs, or in the fire to find relief. John was interrupted from his thoughts when he heard.

"Detective Hammer, what was it like to be a victim, before you became a hero?" one reporter asked him.

"I wasn't the hero, the real hero is standing in the corner over there," John said, as he pointed toward Cindy, standing all alone by the window looking out. "That's the real hero, without my partner's quick thinking. I wouldn't be standing here talking to you now, she's the one you should be questioning," John said.

All the reporters left John and scurried over to Cindy, she looked over at John. John had a very wide smile on his face, and if looks could kill, he'd have a dagger sticking through his heart. Cindy couldn't believe the strength in Austenaco, he picked up Hank, like he was a little kid. Hank had to be at the very least two hundred - twenty pounds and very flexible. She remembered, when Austenaco first told them, that he's been walking in their world for over fifteen or twenty years now. He learned how to speak our language, and rely on eating our foods. He taught himself, and always mixed in when help was needed. Yet nobody seemed to know who he was, and how he's been able to keep his secrete for so long? He seemed to come in, and out of their world with ease, and now he had revenged three, of the five men who killed his family. Cindy now wondered what would happen to Austenaco, after he caught the other two.

Chapter Twelve

It was nearly two weeks, since John or Cindy heard any word, or had any more evidence surfaced, about the other two men who killed Austenaco's family. Believe it or not, John and Cindy felt a bit lonely, without the hearing the big Indian Chief's words of wit, about his old days.

However the news hounds were busy trying to stir up some of their own trouble, as today's headline read. *Chase bank robbery foiled, but police are not revealing how their plan was spoiled.* As the Chief's first statement started, '*With only firing a few shots, Detective's John Hammer and Cindy Sharp, were awarded medals for their bravery. In capturing the thief's, but the only one in the bank at that time, was Detective Hammer. Nothing was ever revealed on how Detective Sharp got into that building, when all the exits were heavily guarded?*'

Captain Phillips, asked his two detectives to come into his office, and after they closed the door behind them. They saw the sweat on the Captains head.

"Hey Captain, what's wrong you look like you're about to faint?" Cindy asked.

"The Mayor wants some answers about this evenings arrests, and if it doesn't sound right. He's threatened, to put us all on foot patrol, if we don't reveal how we spoiled,

that bank heist today. I don't know what to do?" Captain Phillips said.

"When does he want this information Captain?" John asked.

"He wants all of us in his office tomorrow at eight o'clock in the morning, and if he doesn't like what he hears, we could be all walking the beat," Captain Phillips said.

"Captain, can I use my phone?"

"Yes John, but who are you going to call?" Captain Phillips

asked.

"Austenace, maybe he has a way out of this for us, without revealing our real source," John said.

John was happy that he took his answering device, off his cell phone before he gave it to Austenaco. Because it took a whole eight rings, before it would be answered.

"Hello John, it's good to hear from you, have you found anything out about our next guy?"

"No Austenaco, but we do have another problem. Because, of the nagging press wanting answers, on how these crooks were caught, our Mayor is demanding us to explain how we managed to get into the bank. We don't want to tell them about you, so do you have any idea, about what we could do?"

"Yes, John, when do you need, what he's asking for?"

"By eight o'clock tomorrow in the morning."

"Where are you meeting?"

"At his office in the City Hall building located at, 730 Washington Avenue, his name is John Dockett."

"I will be there, and explain to this John Dockett, how this was done."

"Austenaco, I thought you wanted to stay incognito?"

"What does that word mean, I understand many of your words, but some of them I've never head before?"

"Incognito means, you do not, want to be heard of or seen, and that you want to remain a secret. We don't want others like the last five, getting into your world, and causing anymore trouble for you and your people."

"I appreciate your concern John, but I have no intentions of revealing who I really am. I have many different disguises I use, and I will make him believe my story. Your phone is blinking what does that mean?'

"Austenaco, that little charging device I gave you, plug the one end in with the spikes into an electric source, and the other end into the phone. There's a battery that has to be charged every two to five days depending how much it is used. Are you sure you want to meet us tomorrow morning?"

"Do not worry, John, even you may not notice me tomorrow morning. I will see you at

The Mayors office tomorrow, hello, hello," the phone went dead. Austenaco would have to charge the battery.

"Austenaco, are you there?" John asked. Before, it dawned on him that Austenaco's battery must have died on him. He hoped Austenace was right, and he had a plan to get out of this jam. After closing his phone, he turned toward Cindy and Captain Phillips.

"Austenaco, said he has a plan, to get out of this jam, but before he could tell me what he was planning, his phone went dead. Now, we'll have to wait until tomorrow, to find out what is up his sleeve," John said.

"No need for us to worry about it tonight, why don't you two take the rest of the day off with pay. I'm planning on leaving early today myself, we have to get enough sleep and prepare for tomorrow," Captain Phillips said.

"Who can sleep now?' Cindy asked. "Tomorrow will be here, before we blink our eyes, we have to work on, what we're going to say, before we talk to the Mayor."

"I think, we'll have to play it by ear, and see what Austenaco comes up with. After all, he hasn't failed us yet, and I think he's a man of his word. I just wished I knew, how he was going to present himself, without anyone finding out, where he comes from," John said.

"I'd just like to know, how he moves from place to place, without being noticed. He just showed up at the bank, as if he was there all along. I just saw a flash and went to investigate, and that's when I saw him, standing by the side of the building. He took me between a couple slabs of concrete, and the next thing I knew, I was in the basement of the bank. Sometimes I think, he must be a spirit from another world," Cindy said.

"He's not, from another world, just another time, in this world. I just wonder how old he and his people really are, and how long they've been living down there. I checked on what tribe Austenaco was from, and he's from the Cherokee nation tribe. They were known to have lived in Tennessee, Wisconsin, and Nevada mostly. But there were so many tribes of all nationalities, and they intermixed and in time, became just like us. Brothers and sisters through the act of breeding," John said.

"You make it sound like were a bunch of cattle, and not human beings," Cindy said.

"Sometimes, I felt like I'm a puppet on a string, but since we met Austenaco, I came back alive. I forgot what honesty, really felt like, but for some reason, I know he can be trusted," John said.

"I'll wait until tomorrow, to throw in my two cents about that honesty stuff. I'm awful curious, to find out what he plans to do," Cindy said.

"Well there's one thing for sure, we'll find out at eight o'clock tomorrow," John said.

Chapter Thirteen

John was in a deep sound sleep, when his phone started to ring. He checked his clock by the side of his bed, "its 6:30 in the morning, "Who in the hell can that be," he mumbled to himself as he reached for it. "Yes this is John, and this has better be good."

"John, you sound different are you alright?"

"Yes, I was just dreaming of a cool summer sunset, and a lovely lady sitting by my side. Is this Austenaco?"

"Yes my friend, I found out were Ron Saxony is working. You told me if I find anything out, I was to call you before I did anything," Austenaco said.

"Austenaco, don't you ever sleep? What are you planning on doing?" John asked.

"I'm planning on killing him John, and then there's only one left. But first I will meet with you and Cindy later today, and then I will go after this Ron Saxony," he said.

"Austenaco, don't do anything, until we have a chance to talk, if you kill Ron Saxony in front of witnesses. Then you will jeopardize your freedom from our world, you will become a hunted man yourself. Eventually, they will find you, and your existence will no longer be a secret anymore. I know how hard it is to lose a loved one, deep in your heart, but you must think, about your own people, and their freedom from all of this evil," John said.

"That is why I like you John, you speak from the heart. You understand what it means to be different, and I will do as you ask. I will wait until we talk, but don't wait too long. Because, there are many ways of killing someone, without being seen," Austenaco said.

There was a slight pause of silence, and then John said. "See you soon" and hung up the phone.

It was almost eight o'clock John and Cindy were in front of city hall, pacing up and down the sidewalk, waiting for Austenaco to show up. That was until they heard someone say.

"Hey, are you two coming in or what?"

When they turned around, they couldn't believe their eyes, there standing in plan view, and in a tailored suite was Austenaco. He had on a white shirt, with a light blue tie. Navy blue slacks, and a sports coat. He didn't look like he was from another time, and he fit right in to today's society. In the back of John's mind he kept thinking, '*I wonder how many people like Austenaco are walking around our world, in plan sight."* When they walked into the Mayors office, John couldn't keep thinking how different Austenaco looked. After the introduction between (Austenaco) Joe Sebastian, and Mayor John Dockett, the conversation began.

"Hello Mayor Dockett, it's so nice to finally meet you," Austenaco said.

"It's a pleasure meeting you too Mister Sebastian, Not to sound rude or critical. But what are you doing here?" the Mayor asked.

"Detective's John and Cindy, have told me that you want answers, about the recent foiled bank robbery attempt, and I came here to explain what happened" Austenaco said.

"What does the bank robbery have to do with you?" Mayor Dockett asked sternly.

"I was the reason, they were able to access the bank from below, however I can not reveal how, or where we went in. Due to security reasons, if anyone was ever aware of where that secret passage was. How long would you think it would take, before for the bank was robbed again?" Austenaco asked.

"Yes, I suppose you have a valid point Joe, but what am I going to tell the press?"

"Tell them Detective Cindy and I, were down in the basement, when it started, and we were able to hide from the thief's, until it was safe to come out. That was when we put a plan together, and saved those people. It was dumb luck, that we found Detective John Hammer among the hostages first. We were able to free him, which eventually led to our being able to capture those thieves, and save the hostages from harm," Austenaco said.

"That sounds a little far fetched, but it might work. Why do I get a feeling that you're trying to hide something?" Mayor Dockett asked.

"What reason, would we have to lie to you Mayor? I asked the detectives not to mention anything, about my presence because, I'm working undercover you might say, for the bank. The only reason, I wasn't in the bank when they were held up, was because, I was out to lunch, when all of this went down. When I tried to sneak around to enter the hidden entrance, Detective Sharp with her keen sense of wisdom, saw me running toward the back of the bank. If you have to commend someone for their swift actions, I think Detective Cindy Sharp, is the one you should be awarding this certificate," Austenaco said.

"It still sounds like you're trying to hide something, but maybe I'm just being a little paranoid here. Alright Mister Sebastian, I'll tell the newspapers nothing about you. However, I have to warn you, there are a few good reporters here, who might want to push the issue more. Eventually they might find out the truth, but it will never be from me," Mayor Dockett said.

"Thank you Mayor Dockett and we'll cross that bridge, if it ever comes up. It's been a pleasure meeting you, and I hope that someday we can sit down, and maybe have breakfast or dinner together," Austenaco said.

"That would be nice, and Mister Sebastian, if there's anything I can ever help you with, or you need to talk. My door is always open to you," Mayor Dockett said.

With that said, they all shook hands, and departed there own ways. John, Cindy and Austenaco, were chatting and laughing, as they walked through City Hall, but once they opened the front doors and stepped out.

"Nice job, Austenaco, I don't even think, I'm talking to the same guy. You look amazing in that suite, where did you buy that kind of material?" John asked.

"I didn't by it, my cousin shot this big grizzly bear, and my father sewed this suite for me. I bought some of that stuff you call Dye so I could change the original color, and this is what I'm wearing," Austenaco said.

"That explains your coat, but what about your shirt, tie and pants?" Cindy asked.

"Oh, I bought them, with some of the money I received before from John."

"Very impressive, Austenaco, and now back to business. Where is this Ron Saxony supposed to be, so we can go and get him?" Cindy asked

"Someone told me, he owns a warehouse in a big building off of Junction Avenue, and they said, he does import and export service too. I went to check it out, and I was about to make a move on him. Before, you asked me to come here first."

"Do you want to stop someplace first and change, or do you want to go there dressed the way you are?" John asked.

"I figured if I went like this, I wouldn't spook him, and I might be able to get real close to him. I'd become his best friend, stay until close, and then I'd kill him in his own place," Austenaco said.

"Why would you take a chance like that? He might have security guards walking around his place at night," Cindy said.

"I've been watching his place for a while now, and the only thing I've seen. Ron leaves and comes back about an hour later, with a girl wrapped around his arm. After a few hours he leaves, but he always leaves by himself. The girl is nowhere in sight," Austenaco said.

"Maybe there's a back door, he sends them out from," John said.

"Yes, that is a big building, and I wonder how many of those girls, could be spread out across that big vacant building."

"Austenaco, are you saying, you think he could be killing these girls?" John asked.

"Every night, for the past two weeks, he's come back with a girl, and leaves by himself. If that's what he does every night, where are these girls?"

"Without proof, that's just speculation Austenaco, we need something more than just speculation. We have to get inside that building, and check it out, before we do anything else. Because, if he's killing these women, we should nail him to the wall," Cindy said.

"I'm with you on that Cindy, Now if we only had a way to get inside that building, without him seeing us," John said.

"All you have to do is ask me, I'll get you inside that building."

"Should have known but to ask you Austenaco, how many of these building can you really get into?" John asked.

"How many buildings are there in this city?" Austenaco asked.

"Don't have the foggiest notion my friend, but where do we go to get into that building?" John asked.

"There's a little road in the back of that building, and a manhole cover in the middle of the road. Our best bet is to wait until late, so nobody sees us go down it. There's a tunnel that goes left and heads straight to that building," Austenaco said.

"Let's say we pick you up around eight o'clock tonight that should be late enough. Where do you want us to drop you off now?" John asked.

"No need my friends, today I have my own wheels. Pick me up where we first met, when the sun goes down, I'll be waiting."

"Austenaco, never ceases to amaze me. Just when I get a feeling I'm starting to know him, he comes up with something new. I just wonder if he has a driver's license." Cindy said.

Chapter Fourteen

John and Cindy picked up Austenaco, at eight o'clock as planned, and headed to their destination. Austenaco noticed that John and Cindy were dressed differently than before, this was the first time that they weren't dressed in suit pants and vests. Now they were sporting blue jeans and dark color polo shirts, and he was a little curious as to why.

"You two look different from this morning," Austenaco said.

"That's because we're going into a tunnel, and we felt that blue jeans and different shirts were appropriate for this occasion. Besides, since they are dark, it'll be easier to hide if necessary," Cindy said.

"Why do you two always think, that where ever you go, there will be trouble?"

"Because, Austenaco, everyone knows we're police officers, and some people don't take too kindly to our ways of justice. Besides, we're so used to putting protective gear on these days that we feel naked without it." John said.

"We're almost there John, and when you get past the long house on the corner turn left. Go about two houses down, and you should see the cover in the middle of the road."

When they were exiting the car, John opened the trunk to get out the tire iron, to pull the sewer cover off with, but by the time he made it to the hole. Austenaco was standing there holding the cover in his hands, like it was nothing, and as they started down the hole in the ground, and after they were all in, Austenaco put the sewer cover back in place above their heads.

"John, only go halfway down, and then go to your left," Austenaco said.

John, following his instructions as he was told, he was surprised to find another landing in the sewer well. He wondered if anybody working down here had ever noticed it before. After they traveled about fifty yards, the entrance expanded, and they found themselves standing tall. In an area large enough to have them all stand up together and wide enough so they could communicate comfortably, without having to scream.

"How long has that entrance been here?" Cindy asked.

"These tunnels were here, long before your people came along, and before the sewers were put in place, we had to hide the entrances while they dug there own tunnels. But it didn't take them that long, with those big machines they used, and they dug the dirt out and buried long pipes in the ground. I used to watch them when I was younger," Austenaco said.

"Austenaco, there are three entrances which one are we taking?" John asked.

"We'll take the one on the left, and you better let me lead the way. We never know who we might run into in these tunnels, and if they don't know you, they might kill you for trespassing."

Austenaco led the way, and he was moving fast, Cindy, and John were so intrigued in the tunnel, they were having a hard time keeping up with him.

"Hey you two, it's no time for sight seeing, when this is over I will take you through some of the tunnels. But now we have some important business to take care of, before we have fun," Austenaco said.

"You're right my friend, we apologize for our behavior. But what we're looking at impresses the hell out of us, all these years of living, and we never knew these tunnels existed," John said.

"When I was a young brave, my grandfather told me that these were once trenches that were dug into the ground. They were built to keep the dinosaurs away from our village, because many of the dinosaurs didn't have the brains to step up or down. So they would never cross the molts we would dig, and then it happened. The land started to shake, and the sky got so dark, you couldn't see anything but darkness. So we hid underground, and after the trembling stopped. Stepped back outside, and saw the land had changed. The trenches that once were opened were now covered, with land on top of them. At first my people were worried, but when they found out, they could travel underneath the ground. They figured the gods above, gave them a new and safer passage way around the world.

"If you had told me this before, I would have said you were crazy, but now I can't help but believe what you say is true. Which in that case, I must be nuts," John said.

"I'll second that comment John," Cindy said laughing.

"Come on now, it's not that much farther," Austenaco said.

Within about three minutes they were exiting another opening, and this time they were standing in the basement of the old building. John looked back to where they came out, and he couldn't even tell where they came out of. He was amazed at how Austenaco traveled so easily underground, he'd have to come back, and try a few of these tunnels sometime.

When they were walking through the basement, they came upon a strange odor that was sweeping through the basement. Within a few more feet it was really strong, and John with his keen sense of tracking, he had encountered from his days in the army. He was on the trail of a distinct odor, that he knew all too well, from his service days, it was the smell of death.

Before they reached the elevator, the smell was so extreme that Cindy and Austenaco stayed back a little farther. John covered his nose and continued, he had to know if anyone was possibly still alive, before he went on. He opened one of the doors, and saw several girls tied up with chains. It was too late to save any of them, and they had to have been there for quite sometime. He continued and after three more doors he was about to call it quits, before he heard a faint cry for help. It was two more doors down, and he heard the whimpering of a female voice. He opened the door, and not only found one girl alive but four. He called back to Cindy and Austenaco to bring some water, and then he helped the girls get out of their hand cuffs.

"Thank you mister, we don't know who you are, or how you found us, but thank you," the blonde said.

"Stay quite a minute, save your strength. This isn't quite over yet, how did you get down here?" John asked.

"This guy calls us out to be his date, and after he wines and dines us, he asks us over to his place. When we get here, there's another guy in the place, and when we say no to doing what they want us to do. They beat us, and then chain us up down here, as you can see not very many girls said yes. From time to time, he'll come down with his friend, and take one of the weaker girls, and force them to do what they want,"

"Has anyone ever tried to escape?" John asked.

"Yes there was one girl she faked how weak she was. When they unlocked her cuffs, and took her out of the room, she kicked and hit her way out. If not for that damn old elevator, she probably would have made it. When they caught her, they brought her back. They beat her... like I never saw anyone get beat before, and I think they broke every bone in her body. They knew what they were doing too. Because, she was still alive before they finally let her die. They just sat back, and we all had to us watch her die, a slow and painful death." The Blonde girl said.

"I'd like to rip their hearts out of their chests, they don't deserve to live," Austenaco said.

One by one, they released all the girls, and helped them get their strength back in their arms and legs. Cindy suddenly winced, as she noticed one of the women hanging in the room. She ran over there like a cougar after her cub, and said Trish, Trish, but she knew she wouldn't be answering back.

"Sorry Cindy, a friend of yours?" John asked.

"No she was one of my contacts, I used to use when I first started as a cop, I thought she had cleaned up her act, and took herself off the streets. I guess she's off the streets now, what a waste, and she was such a smart girl. Apparently not smart enough to avoid the streets."

"Don't blame her Cindy we're not all street girls, But we are girls, who have nobody else to turn too. Three or four of the women were college students, before they took them," the Blonde girl said.

"What's your name?" Cindy asked.

"My name is Monica Johnson, and I've been here, I think three weeks now. What day is it?"

"It's April 15, 2013," John said.

"My god, I've been here almost six weeks, my parents must be really worried about me by now," Monica said.

"Don't worry Monica, after we have you checked out at the hospital, you'll be back with your families again. In fact, we'll let you call them on the way, but now we have some unfinished business to take care off," John said.

After surveying the tragedy they saw was happening in this building, John turned to Austenaco with tears in his eyes. Austenaco knew what John was saying, without even saying a word. He started putting on his war paint, and then they heard some commotion by the elevator shaft.

"Monica, I think you're friends are back, you girls get back into the room. We'll be right here behind them, and please don't panic," John said.

"I'm getting in the room with them John, let's see what they do when they see a .45 staring them in the face as they open the door," Cindy said.

"No time to argue here they come," John said.

When John looked over at Austenaco, he saw a look on his face that scared him to death. John knew, Austenaco, was hurting once again inside. Austenaco cherished life, and he condemned the ones who would take a life. John knew that no matter what he said, to Austenaco would fall on deaf ears. There was only one thing on Austenaco mind, and that was killing these men who have caused so much pain.

There was dead silence, as they heard the elevator stop, and the wood doors open up. They were dragging someone behind them, and when they came to the locked doors. One of them noticed the skid marks on the ground, but he must have thought that was from the last time they were down here. I think they turned a shade of grey, when they opened up the door, and saw Cindy holding her gun, aiming it between their eyes.

"Alright, you scum bags, back up nice and slow, turn around lace your fingers behind your heads, and kneel down on the ground," she said.

"I don't believe you'll shoot, in fact I don't even think your gun is loaded," the little man said.

Cindy proceeded to lower her gun, and shot him in the knee cap, "Are you convinced now, yes that it's loaded?"

"You bitch, I'm going to kill you," he said.

"Alright which one of you is named Ron Saxony?" she asked.

"Who wants to know bitch?" the taller one asked.

Cindy shot him in the knee cap too. "I don't like that kind of language, I'm sorry about your knee, it's a nervous twitch I have, when ever someone calls me a bitch."

"Cindy, don't kill him before I get a chance to have some fun," Austenaco said as he walked out of the shadows of the room.

Both men saw the look in his eyes, and started to shake like a mixed drink. They remembered him from behind the rocks, but now he looked a lot bigger to them.

"Hey I'm sorry about your wife, I tried to stop them but they wouldn't listen to me,"

The shorter one said.

"What is you name?" Austenaco asked.

"Phil Rush is my name, and I had nothing to do with, murdering your wife."

"I believe you Phil, but you did drive the car, and that makes you just as guilty as if you killed them yourself."

"What do you mean them, who else did they kill?" Phil asked.

"My little six year old boy was in her arms, when Ron shot her in the head, the bullet went through her, and into my son's head. Killing them both, and because you told me the truth, I will kill you last," Austenaco said.

"You can't kill us we have rights, we have a right to have a jury trial," the taller one said.

"What name do you go by sir?" John asked.

"I'm not talking without my lawyer," he said.

"To bad Ron, we already know your name. I just wanted to know, if you'd be as courteous as your friend there, but if you insist on being a hard ass. I guess there's nothing else we need from you," John said.

When Austenaco made a step toward Ron, he opened up like a baby. "Yes my name is Ron Saxony, and I was there when your wife was killed. I'm very sorry for that. Now can we get out of here, so I can beat this rap, and be out again in a few months."

"You know what amazes me Ron, its guy's like you who think it's so easy to kill someone, and get away with it. I told Austenaco before we arrived here, not to take the law into his own hands, but after seeing, what you've put these poor ladies through. I've changed my mind, for you see my partner Cindy there, was very close to a few of the women that you've killed in these rooms. So we will be your judge and jury down here, we've already heard from both sides of the cases now. You ladies who are still alive how do you plea? Thumbs up for live, thumbs down for kill," John asked.

They were startled when not only the four women they rescued voted, but two women in another room were still barley alive. While Cindy went to check on them, John looked over at Austenaco.

When Ron saw John nod his head at Austenaco, he tried to make a run for it. Before Ron could get to the gate of the elevator, he felt a sharp pain in his right leg, and when he looked down, he saw a big knife sticking out of his right thigh. Austenaco walked up slowly to him. Grabbing the knife handle, he pushed it further into his leg, and then he hit Ron with a right fist. Ron was bleeding from his nose, and shaking when the big Indian, stood there and snarled at him. Ron tried a desperation kick with his left leg, but when he stuck it out toward the Indian. Austenaco grabbed his leg, and without much trouble, flung him back against the wall. Ron was thrown so hard, that when he hit the wall, he indented the dirt wall. Ron was seeing stars, as he tried to stand up on his feet. After he regained some of his senses, he was like a charging wounded bull, as he ran toward the Indian. Austenaco was surprised, when Ron bent down and chopped him in his knee cap. Austenaco went down with pain, he tried to stand up, and when Ron saw him favoring the leg he just hit. Ron went at the same leg again, but this time when he dove for the leg. Austenaco brought his big foot straight up, and caught Ron square in the face. Austenaco lost his balance a little, but now, Ron's nose and mouth were bleeding like a waterfall. Ron tasted his own blood as it ran down from his nose, and then Ron came after Austenaco again. He tried to give him a straight boot in the chest, but Austenaco side stepped the kick. He grabbed his foot as he went by, and as quick as a cat stuck his left leg in between two of the pillars in the basement. Austenaco, pulled his leg sideways with tremendous power against a pillar, and all they heard was a big crack, followed by a loud scream. Austenaco tore his leg almost completely off his body, as his leg just dangled in mid air.

Austenaco told John he wanted to tear him apart limb from limb, and that's exactly what was happening at this point. John for a split minute felt sorry for Ron, until he looked over, and saw the other two other women, Cindy had just pulled out of the other cell. They looked very undernourished, and could barley stand let alone walk. His temper flared up once again, and he found himself yelling Austenaco on.

"Make him pay the hard way Austenaco, tear that bastard apart," John yelled.

With the knife still in his right leg, and now his left leg shattered. Ron could no longer stand, and when he tried to use his arms for help. Austenaco just broke them too. With Ron completely immobilized, Austenaco looked over at Phil. When he saw Phil's head was wet with sweat, and his eyes were full of fear. Austenaco knew that now was a good opportunity, to see just how sorry Phil really was.

"Do you want to live little man?" Austenaco asked Phil.

"Yes, tell me what to do I'll do anything," Phil said.

Austenaco handed Phil a gun, with one bullet in the chamber, "Kill your friend and you can go. But say nothing about what happened here, if you say anything about me. I will come after you, and make you pay like your friend here," Austenaco said.

When Phil didn't make a move, John said. "Phil it's not often that Austenaco lets someone live, but you have to prove to him, that you didn't approve of what Ron did to his family. You have only two choices here, either you kill Ron now, or you join him in the same condition he's in now. Except for one different thing, Austenaco will make it so you die real slow. Which means you'll be in so much pain, that you'll beg us to kill you. But he will not be as merciful as he is now, you will die a slow and painful death.

After Phil heard his choices, he picked up the gun. He walked over to Ron, and whispered I'm sorry Ron. He pointed the gun at his head, and pulled the trigger, and after he shot Ron he turned around and found himself all alone. Everyone was gone, but where did they go. Then he herd the sirens out in the back, and as he tried to get away. He forgot about his wounded leg, and when he tried to stand up he couldn't walk. Austenaco let him live, but he wasn't going to be free. The police came in and went straight to the basement, and they arrested Phil for the murder of not only the women, but also of his partner too.

Chapter Fifteen

When Captain Phillips returned back to his precinct, he saw John, Cindy and Austenaco standing around talking and laughing. He motioned for them to go into his office, and they obediently walked right in, and sat down.

"I saw the kind of work you did on those goons, and even though I don't really approve of the way it was done. I must say I'm happy that we finally nailed these clowns, Austenaco, I don't know how, but I do know why you're involved with this mess, but it was nice to have your assistance when we needed it," Captain Phillips said.

"I had a vendetta against these men too Captain Phillips, they invaded our territory, and killed my wife and son. I'm sorry if I caused anyone any hardship, but I did what I had to do. I'm thankful for all your help along the way, and my heart is broken because I lost a family. But it has been slightly repaired by your new friendship, and I can go back now and be among my people. I will tell them about how brave you are up here, and if they ever need any help, to call on John or Cindy or even you Captain," Austenaco said.

"Austenaco, I was asked before about making you a bounty hunter for us, so you can help us track and locate the bad guys. I think it would be a splendid Idea, and I'm glad to offer you such a contract," Captain Phillips said.

"John, I thought you said you had someone else you wanted to go after. Wasn't his name Alvino Ruiz?" Austenaco asked.

"Not yet Austenaco, your job is done now. He's not the one we were after, but soon he will slip up and then he'll be ours. You said you didn't want my phone, if we need you, how, are we supposed to get a hold of you?"

"I do not need a phone for you to contact me. I will know when you're in trouble, and I will be there to help you, when the time is right. We've been walking in your world, for as long as we've been alive, and when the time is right. We will cross paths once again, until then my friends stay true to your heart. Just remember one thing before I leave you now. You were never alone, and you will never be alone. Someone is always watching you.

John was taking Cindy home in his car, when he asked her. "Would you like to stop by my place for a nightcap partner?"

"What else are we going to do besides talk?"

"Anything you want my dear, and if you want to sit on my lap. We can talk about the first thing that's pops up," John said.

When they entered John's house, he went to reach for the light switch. Cindy grabbed his hand and asked, "I've seen enough bright lights tonight. Do you have any candles?"

"Sorry I'm a bachelor I don't have any candles,"

That's alright, on second thought John, who needs candles? We'll make our own flames tonight," Cindy said and led John into the bedroom

"You know Cindy, this could get complicated."

THE END

CHARACTERS

Detective: John Hammer

Detective: Cindy Sharp

Detective: Sam Stone

Detective: Mary Chauffer

Detective: Sidney Sneed

Detective: Pete Ochowa

Captain: Stephen Phillips

Evidence Boss: Slim Stickman

Lab Technician: Shirley Jacobs

Professor: Albert Goodyear Archaeologist for Paloe Indians Prehistoric times

Coroner: Dr. Phyllis Hartman

Forensic Team: Sergeant Harry Meyer

Forensic Team: Sergeant Curt Clemente

Forensic Team: Sergeant Sandy Bellows

Chief: Austenaco (Alias John Sebastian)

Chief: Yonaguska Head chief

Warrior: Salai- Squirrel

Warrior: Chea Sequal-Red Bird

Warrior: Waya- Wolf

Squaw: Awinta- Fawn

Squaw: Leotie- Flower of Prairie

Squaw: Tsula-Fox

Squaw- Hialeah- Beautiful Meadow

Bad Guy-Billy Winters

Bad Guy- Charles White

Bad Guy- Jeff Jenkins

Bartender- Charlie

Negotiator- Rick King

Mobster Alvin Ruiz

Bank Robber- Jerry

Bank Robber- Kevin

Bank Robber- Roger

Bad Guy- Ron Saxony

Bad Guy- Phil Rush

Mayor – John Dickert

www.ingramcontent.com/pod-product-compliance
Lightning Source LLC
LaVergne TN
LVHW040156080526
838202LV00042B/3186